The Adventures of JONATHAN GULLIBLE
A Free Market Odyssey

By Ken Schoolland
Third, revised and expanded edition, 2001 ©

Illustrations by Randall Lavarias

An Educational Publication of
Small Business Hawaii

Twice awarded the
GEORGE WASHINGTON HONOR MEDALS
from the Freedoms Foundation at Valley Forge
for Economic Education and Public Communication

Dedicated to my daughter,
Kenli

Published in more than twenty international languages: English, Russian, Dutch, Norwegian, Lithuanian, Romanian, Serbian, Croatian, Macedonian, Slovenian, German, Spanish, Palauan, Chinese, Albanian, Latvian, Portuguese, Hungarian, Italian, Romany, Czech, Japanese, and Polish.

Published by Small Business Hawaii, Hawaii Kai Corporate Plaza, 6600 Kalanianaole Hwy., Suite 212, Honolulu, Hawaii, 96825, USA, (808) 396-1724 phone, (808) 396-1726 FAX, email: sbh@lava.net, website: www.smallbusinesshawaii.org.

ISBN: 0-9623467-2-1

Printed by Edward Enterprises, Inc.

CONTENTS

PROLOGUE

 n accordance with Mr. Gullible's wishes, I take up the task of recounting a bizarre tale that he related to me in his last years. I have made every effort to remain true to his account, despite some literary license. Included are a few of his sketches, firsthand testimony about the people and incidents of his journey.

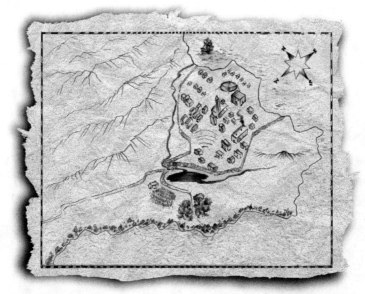

CHAPTER 1

A GREAT STORM

n a sunny seaside town, long before it filled up with movie stars driving convertibles, there lived a young man named Jonathan Gullible. He was unremarkable to anyone except his parents, who thought him clever, sincere, and remarkably athletic—from the top of his tousled sandy-brown head to the bottoms of his oversized feet. They worked hard in a small chandler's shop on the main street of a town that was home to a busy fishing fleet. It had a fair number of hard-working folk, some good, some bad, and mostly just plain average.

When he wasn't doing chores or errands for his family's store, Jonathan would steer his rough sailboat out the narrow channel of a small boat harbor in search of adventure. Like many youths spending their early years in the same place, Jonathan found life a little dull and thought the people around him unimaginative. He longed to see a strange ship or sea serpent on his brief voyages beyond the channel. Maybe he would run into a pirate ship and be forced to sail the seven seas as part of the crew. Or, perhaps, a whaler on the prowl for oily prey would let him on board for the hunt. Most sailings, however, ended when his stomach pinched with hunger or his throat parched with thirst and the thought of supper was the only thing on his mind.

On one of those fine spring days, when the air was as crisp as a sun-dried sheet, the sea looked so good that Jonathan thought nothing of packing his lunch and fishing gear into his little boat for a cruise. As he tacked beyond the rocky point of the lighthouse, he felt as free-spirited as the great condor that he watched soaring above the coastal mountains. With his back to the breeze, Jonathan didn't notice the dark storm clouds gathering on the horizon.

Jonathan had only recently begun to sail beyond the mouth of the harbor, but he was getting more confident. When the wind began to pick up strength, he didn't worry until it was too late. Soon he was struggling frantically at the rigging as the storm broke over him with violent force. His boat tossed dizzily among the waves like a cork in a tub. Every effort he made to control his vessel failed, useless against the tremendous winds. At last, he dropped to the bottom of the boat, clutching the sides and hoping that he would not capsize. Night and day blended together in a terrifying swirl.

When the storm finally died, his boat was a shambles, its mast broken, sails torn, and it tipped in a definite list to starboard. The sea calmed but a thick fog lingered, shrouding his craft and cutting off any view. After drifting for days his water ran out and he could only moisten his lips on the condensation that dripped off the shreds of canvas. Then the fog lifted and Jonathan spotted the faint outline of an island. As he drifted closer, he made out unfamiliar headlands jutting from sandy beaches and steep hillsides covered by lush vegetation.

The waves carried him onto a shallow reef. Abandoning his craft, Jonathan swam eagerly to shore. He quickly found and devoured the pink guavas, ripe bananas and other delicious fruit that flourished beyond the narrow sandy beach in the humid jungle climate. As soon as he regained some strength, Jonathan felt desolate but relieved to be alive. He actually grew excited at his unintended plunge into adventure. He immediately set off along the white sand beach to discover more about this strange new land.

CHAPTER 2

TROUBLEMAKERS

onathan walked for several hours without a glimpse of any sign of life. Suddenly, something moved in the thicket and a small animal with a yellow-striped tail flashed down a barely visible track. "A cat," thought Jonathan. "Maybe it will lead me to other life." He dived through the thick foliage.

Just as he lost sight of the beach and was deep in the jungle, he heard a sharp scream. He stopped, cocked his head, and tried to locate the source of the sound. Directly ahead, he heard another shrill cry for help. Pushing up an incline and through a mass of branches and vines, he clawed his way forward and stumbled onto a wider path.

As he rounded a sharp bend in the trail, Jonathan ran full tilt into the side of a burly man. "Out of my way, runt!" bellowed the man, brushing him aside like a gnat. Dazed, Jonathan looked up and saw two men dragging a young woman, kicking and yelling, down the trail. By the time he caught his breath, the trio had disappeared. Certain that he couldn't free the woman alone, Jonathan ran back down the trail looking for help.

A clearing opened and he saw a group of people gathered around a big tree—beating it with sticks. Jonathan ran up and grabbed the arm of a man who was obviously the supervisor. "Please sir, help!" gasped Jonathan. "Two men have captured a woman and she needs help!"

"Don't be alarmed," the man said gruffly. "She's under arrest. Forget her and move along, we've got work to do."

"Arrest?" said Jonathan, still huffing. "She didn't look like, uh, like a criminal." Jonathan wondered, if she was guilty, why did she cry so desperately for help? "Pardon me, sir, but what was her crime?"

"Huh?" snorted the man with irritation. "Well, if you must know, she threatened the jobs of everyone working here."

"She threatened people's jobs? How'd she do that?" asked Jonathan.

Glaring down at his ignorant questioner, the supervisor motioned for Jonathan to come over to a tree where workers busily pounded away at the trunk. Proudly, he said, "We are tree workers. We knock down trees for wood by beating them with these sticks. Sometimes a hundred people, working round-the-clock, can knock down a good-sized tree in less than a month." The man pursed his lips and carefully brushed a speck of dirt from the sleeve of his handsomely cut coat.

He continued, "That Drawbaugh woman came to work this morning with a sharp piece of metal attached to the end of her stick. She cut down a tree in less than an hour—all by herself! Think of it! Such an outrageous threat to our traditional employment had to be stopped."

Jonathan's eyes widened, aghast to hear that this woman was punished for her creativity. Back home, everyone used axes and saws for cutting trees. That's how he got the wood for his own boat. "But her invention," exclaimed Jonathan, "allows people of all sizes and strengths to cut down trees. Won't that make it faster and cheaper to get wood and make things?"

"What do you mean?" the man said angrily. "How could anyone encourage an idea like that? This noble work can't be done by any weakling who comes along with some new idea."

"But sir," said Jonathan, trying not to offend, "these good tree workers have talented hands and brains. They could use the time saved from knocking down trees to do other things. They could make tables, cabinets, boats, or even houses!"

"Listen, you," the man said with a menacing look, "the purpose of work is to have full and secure employment—not new products." The tone of his voice turned ugly. "You sound like some kind of troublemaker. Anyone who supports that infernal woman is trouble. Where are you from?"

Jonathan replied anxiously, "I don't even know Miss Drawbaugh and I don't mean any trouble, sir. I'm sure you're right. Well, I must be going." With that, Jonathan turned back the way he came, hurrying down the path. His first encounter with the people of the island left him feeling very nervous.

CHAPTER 3

A COMMONS TRAGEDY

he trail widened a bit as it cut through the dense jungle. The midday sun burned hot overhead when Jonathan found a small lake. As he scooped up some water to refresh himself, Jonathan heard someone's voice warning, "I wouldn't drink the water if I were you."

Jonathan looked around and saw an old man kneeling at the shore, cleaning a few tiny fish on a plank. Beside him were a basket, reel, and three poles propped in the mud, each dangling a line in the water. "Is the fishing good?" inquired Jonathan politely.

Without bothering to look up, the man replied, somewhat crossly, "Nope. These little critters were all I got today." He proceeded to fillet the fish and to drop them into a hot skillet that was set over a smoldering fire. The fish sizzling in the pan smelled delicious. Jonathan spotted the rough yellow-striped cat that he had followed already picking at scraps of fish. His mouth watered.

Jonathan, who considered himself an accomplished fisherman, asked, "What did you use for bait?"

The man looked up at Jonathan thoughtfully. "Ain't nothing wrong with my bait, sonny. I've caught the best of what's left in this here lake."

Sensing a solitary mood in this fisherman, Jonathan thought he might learn more by just remaining silent awhile. Eventually, the old fisherman beckoned him to sit beside the fire to share some fish and a little bread. Jonathan devoured his meal hungrily, though he felt guilty about taking a portion of this man's meager lunch. After they finished, Jonathan kept quiet and, sure enough, the old man began to talk.

"Years ago there were some really big fish to catch here," the man said wistfully. "But they've all been caught. Now the little ones are all that's left."

"But the little ones will grow, won't they?" asked Jonathan. He stared at the lush grasses growing in the shallow waters along the shore where many fish might lurk.

"Nah. People take all the fish, even the little ones. Not only that, people dump garbage into the far end of the lake. See that thick scum along the far side?"

Jonathan looked perplexed. "Why do others take your fish and dump trash in your lake?"

"Oh, no," said the fisherman, "this isn't my lake. It belongs to everyone—just like the forests and the streams."

"These fish belong to everyone..." Jonathan paused, "including me?" He began to feel a little less guilty about sharing a meal that he had no part in making.

"Not exactly," the man replied. "What belongs to everyone really belongs to no one—that is, until a fish bites my hook. Then it's mine."

"I don't get it," said Jonathan, frowning in confusion. Half speaking to himself, he repeated, "The fish belong to everyone, which means that they really belong to no one, until one bites your hook. Then, the fish is yours? But do you do anything to take care of the fish or to help them grow?"

"Of course, not," the man said with a snort of derision. "Why should I care for the fish just so someone else can come over here at any time and catch 'em? If someone else gets the fish or pollutes the lake with garbage, then there goes all my effort!"

With a mournful glance at the water, the old fisherman added sadly, "I wish I really did own the lake. Then I'd make sure that the fish were well tended. I'd care for the lake just like the cattleman who manages the ranch over in the next valley. I'd breed the strongest, fattest fish and you can bet that no fish rustlers or garbage dumpers would get past me. I'd make sure..."

"Who manages the lake now?" interrupted Jonathan.

The weathered face of the fisherman grew hard. "The lake is run by the Council of Lords. Every four years, the Lords are elected to the Council. Then the Council appoints a manager and pays him from my taxes. The fish manager is supposed to watch out for too much fishing and dumping. Funny thing is, friends of the Lords get to fish and dump as they please."

The two sat and watched the wind stir a pattern of ripples across the silver lake. Jonathan noticed the yellow cat sitting erect, sniffing and staring at a fish head on his plate. He tossed the head and the cat caught it neatly with one hooked paw. This feline looked tough, with one ear torn from some old battle.

Mulling the old fisherman's tale, Jonathan asked, "Is the lake well-managed?"

"See for yourself," the old fisherman grumbled. "Look at the size of my puny catch. Seems like the fish get smaller as the manager's salary gets bigger."

CHAPTER 4

THE FOOD POLICE

Paths converged with the dirt trail as it broadened into a gravelly country road. Instead of jungle, Jonathan passed rolling pastures and fields of ripening crops and rich orchards. The sight of all that food growing reminded Jonathan of how little he had eaten for lunch. He detoured toward a neat white farmhouse, hoping to find his bearings and maybe another meal.

On the front porch, he found a young woman and a small boy huddled together crying. "Excuse me," said Jonathan awkwardly. "Is there any trouble?"

The woman looked up, eyes wet with tears. "It's my husband. Oh, my husband!" she wailed. "I knew one day it would come to this. He's been arrested," she sobbed, "by the Food Police!"

"I'm very sorry to hear about that, ma'am. Did you say 'Food Police'?" asked Jonathan. He patted the dark head of the boy sympathetically. "Why did they arrest him?"

The woman gritted her teeth, fighting to hold back tears. Scornfully, she said, "His crime was that of growing too much food!"

Jonathan was shocked. This island was truly a strange place! "It's a crime to grow too much food?"

The woman continued, "Last year the Food Police issued orders telling him how much food he could produce and sell to the country folk. They told us that low prices hurt the other farmers." She bit her lip slightly, then blurted out, "My husband was a better farmer than all the rest of them put together!"

Instantly Jonathan heard a sharp roar of laughter behind him. A heavyset man strutted up the walk from the road to the farmhouse. "Ha!" he sneered, "I say that the best farmer is the one who gets the farm. Right?" With a grand sweep of his hand, the man glared at the woman and her son and commanded, "Now get your things packed and out of here! The Council of Lords has awarded this land to me."

The man grabbed up a toy dog that was lying on the steps and thrust it into Jonathan's hands. "I'm sure she can use the help, bud. Get moving, this is my place now."

The woman stood up, eyes snapping in anger, "My husband was a better farmer than you'll ever be."

"That's a matter of debate," the man chuckled rudely. "Oh sure, he had a green thumb. And he was a genius at figuring what to plant and how to please his customers. Quite a man! But he forgot one thing—the Council of Lords sets the prices and crops. And the Food Police enforce the Council rules."

"You parasite!" yelled the woman. "You always guess wrong, you waste good manure and seed on everything you plant, and no one wants to buy what you grow. You plant in a flood plain or on parched clay and it never matters if you lose everything. You just get the Council of Lords to pay for the rot. They've even paid you to destroy entire crops."

Jonathan frowned, "There's no advantage in being a good farmer?"

"Being a good farmer is a handicap," answered the woman as her face reddened. "My husband, unlike this toad, refused to flatter the Lords and tried to produce honest crops and real sales."

Shoving the woman and her boy off the porch, the man growled, "Enough! He refused to follow the annual quotas. No one bucks the Food Police and gets away with it. Now get off *my* land!"

Jonathan helped the woman carry her belongings. The woman and her son walked slowly away from their former home. At a bend in the road, all turned to take one last look at the neat house and barn. "What will happen to you now?" asked Jonathan.

The woman sighed, "I can't afford to pay the high food prices. Luckily, we've got relatives and friends to rely on for help. Otherwise, I could beg the Council of Lords to take care of Davy and me. They'd like that," she muttered bitterly. She took the young boy's hand and picked up a large bundle saying, "Come along, Davy."

Jonathan gripped his stomach—now feeling a little more sick than hungry.

CHAPTER 5

CANDLES AND COATS

onathan accompanied the despairing woman and her boy a couple miles down the road to the home of her relatives. They thanked him warmly and invited him to stay. One look told him that the house could barely contain the whole family, so he excused himself and continued on his way.

The road took him to a river where he found a bridge to a walled town on the other side. The narrow bridge held an imposing divider. On the right-hand side of the bridge, a sign pointed to the town reading, "ENTER STULTA CITY, ISLE OF CORRUMPO." On the other side of the divider, another sign simply read, "EXIT ONLY, DO NOT ENTER."

That was not the oddest feature of the bridge. To cross into town, one had to climb over jagged obstacles. Piles of sharp rocks and massive boulders blocked the entire entry side of the bridge. Several travelers had dropped their parcels by the way or into the river rather than haul them over the craggy barrier. Others, especially the elderly, simply turned back. Behind one feeble traveler, Jonathan spied the familiar yellow-striped cat with a ragged right ear, sniffing and pawing at a bundle that had been discarded. As he watched, the cat extracted a piece of dried meat from the torn bundle.

In contrast, the exit side of the bridge was smooth and clear. Merchants carrying goods out of town departed with ease. Jonathan wondered, "Why to they make it so tough to get into this place while it is so easy to get out?"

Jonathan clambered over the entrance side of the bridge, slipping on the uneven footing and hauling himself up on the boulders. He finally arrived at a pair of thick wooden gates that were thrown wide open to allow him to pass through the great town wall. People riding horses, people carrying boxes and bundles, and people driving all manner of wagons and carts traversed the roads inside. Jonathan straightened his shoulders, dusted off his tattered shirt and pants and marched through the gateway. The cat slipped in behind him.

Just inside, a woman, holding a rolled parchment, sat behind a table that was covered with bright little medallions. "Please," asked the woman, giving a wide smile and reaching out to pin one of the medallions onto Jonathan's shirt pocket, "won't you sign my petition?"

"Well, I don't know," stammered Jonathan. I wonder if you could direct me toward the center of town?"

The woman eyed him suspiciously. "You don't know the town?"

Jonathan hesitated, noting the chilly tone that had crept into her voice. Quickly, he said, "And where do I sign your petition?"

The woman smiled again. "Sign just below the last name, right here. You're helping so many people with this."

Jonathan shrugged his shoulders and took up her pen. He felt sorry for her, sitting all bundled in heavy clothing, sweating profusely on such a pleasant, sunny day. "What's this petition for?" asked Jonathan.

She clasped her hands in front of her as if preparing to sing a solo. "This is a petition to protect jobs and industry. You are in favor of jobs and industry, are you not?" she pleaded.

"Of course I am," said Jonathan, remembering the enterprising young woman who was arrested for threatening the jobs of tree workers. The last thing he wanted was to sound disinterested in people's work.

"How will this help?" asked Jonathan as he scribbled his name badly enough so that no one could possibly read it.

"The Council of Lords protects our local industries from products that come from outside of town. As you can see, we've made progress with our bridge, but there's so much more to be done. If enough people sign my petition, the Lords have promised to ban foreign items that hurt my industry."

"What is your industry?" asked Jonathan.

The woman declared proudly, "I represent the makers of candles and coats. This petition calls for a ban on the sun."

"The sun?" gasped Jonathan. "How, uh, why ban the sun?"

She eyed Jonathan defensively. "I know it sounds a bit drastic, but don't you see—the sun hurts candle makers and coat makers. People don't buy candles and coats when they're warm and have light. Surely you realize that the sun is a very cheap source of foreign light and heat. Well, this just cannot be tolerated!"

"But light and heat from the sun are free," protested Jonathan.

The woman looked hurt and whined, "That's the problem, don't you see?" Taking out a little pad and pencil, she tried to draw a few notations for him. "According to my calculations, the low-cost availability of these foreign elements reduces potential employment and wages by at least fifty percent—that is, in the industries which I represent. A heavy tax on windows, or maybe an outright prohibition, should improve this situation nicely."

Jonathan put down her petition. "But if people pay for light and heat, then they will have less money to spend on other things—things like meat or drink or bread."

"I don't represent the butchers, or the brewers, or the bakers," the woman said brusquely. Sensing a change in Jonathan's attitude, she snatched away the petition. "Obviously you are more interested in some consumer whim than in protecting the security of jobs and sound business investment. Good day to you," she said, ending the conversation abruptly.

Jonathan backed away from the table. "Ban the sun?" he thought. "What crazy ideas! First hatchets and food, then the sun. What will they think of next?"

CHAPTER 6

THE TALL TAX

As Jonathan strode through the town he immediately noticed a dignified well-dressed man kneeling in the street, trying painfully to walk. Yet, the man didn't appear to be crippled—just short. Jonathan offered a helping hand, but the man brushed him aside.

"No, thank you!" said the man, wincing in pain. "I can walk okay. Using knees takes some getting used to."

"You're okay? But why don't you get off your knees and walk on your feet?"

"Ooooh!" moaned the man, squirming in discomfort. "It's a minor adjustment to the tax code."

"The tax code?" repeated Jonathan. "What's the tax code have to do with walking?"

"Everything! Ow!" By now the man settled back on his heels, resting from his torturous ordeal. He pulled a handkerchief from his shirt pocket and mopped his brow. He shifted his balance to massage one knee, then the other. Many layers of worn-out patches had been sewn on at the knees. "The tax code," he said, "has recently been amended to level the field for people of different heights."

"Level the field?" asked Jonathan.

"Please stoop over so I don't have to shout," pleaded the man. "That's better. The Council of Lords decided that tall people have too many advantages."

"Advantages of tallness?"

"Oh, yes! Tall people are always favored in hiring, promotion, sports, entertainment, politics, and even marriage! Ooooh!" He wrapped the handkerchief around the newest of many rips in his gray pants. "So the Lords decided to level us with a stiff tallness tax."

"Tall people get taxed?" Jonathan glanced sideways and felt his posture begin to droop.

"We're taxed in direct proportion to our height."

"Did anyone object?" asked Jonathan.

"Only those who refused to get on their knees," the man said. "Of course, we've allowed an exemption for politicians. We usually vote tall! We like to look up to our leaders."

Jonathan was dumbfounded. By now he found himself slouching, self-consciously trying to shrink. With both hands pointing down at the man's knees he questioned incredulously, "You'll walk on your knees just for a tax break?"

"Sure!" replied the man in a pained voice. "Our whole lives are shaped to fit the tax code. There are some who have even started to crawl."

"Wow! That must hurt!" Jonathan exclaimed.

"Yeah, but it hurts more not to. Ow! Only fools stand erect and pay the higher taxes. So, if you want to act smart, get on your knees. It'll cost you plenty to stand tall."

Jonathan looked around to see a handful of people walking on their knees. One woman across the street was slowly crawling. Many people scurried about half-crouching, their shoulders hunched over. Only a few walked proudly erect, ignoring the sanctions completely. Then Jonathan caught sight of three gentlemen across the street sitting on a park bench. "Those three men," indicated Jonathan. "Why are they covering their eyes, ears, and mouths?"

"Oh, them? They're practicing," replied the man as he leaned forward on his knees to shuffle along. "Getting ready for a new series of tax proposals."

CHAPTER 7

BEST LAID PLANS

Dull two- and three-story wooden row houses lined the streets of the town. Then Jonathan noticed one grand, elegant home, standing apart from everything, isolated on an expansive green lawn. It looked solidly built, adorned with attractive latticework and freshly-painted white walls.

Curious, Jonathan approached the house and found a crew wielding heavy sticks, attacking the rear of the home and trying to tear it down. They weren't very enthusiastic and moved very slowly at the job. Nearby, a dignified, gray-haired woman stood with her hands clenched, visibly unhappy at the proceedings. She groaned audibly when a piece of the wall came down.

Jonathan walked over to her and asked, "That house looks well-built. Who's the owner?"

"That's a good question!" the woman shot back vehemently. "I thought I owned this house."

"You *thought* you owned it? Surely you know if you own a house," said Jonathan.

The ground shook as the entire rear wall collapsed inside. The woman stared miserably at the cloud of dust billowing up from the rubble. "It's not that simple," yelled the woman over the noise. "Ownership is control, right? But who controls this house? The Lords control everything—so they're the real owners of this house, even though I built it and paid for every board and nail."

Growing more agitated, she walked over and ripped a paper off a single post left where a whole wall had stood moments before. "See this notice?" She crumpled it, threw it down and stamped on it. "The officials tell me what I may build, how I may build, when I may build, and what I can use it for. Now they tell me they're tearing it down. Does that sound like I own the property?"

"Well," ventured Jonathan sheepishly, "didn't you live in it?"

"Only so long as I could keep paying the property taxes. If I didn't pay, the officials would have booted me out faster than you can say 'next case'!" The woman grew red with fury and continued breathlessly, "No one really owns anything. We merely rent from the Council so long as we pay their taxes."

"You didn't pay the tax?" asked Jonathan.

"Of course I paid the cursed tax!" the woman practically shouted.

"But that wasn't enough for them. This time, the Lords said that my plan for the house didn't fit their plan—the master plan of 'superior owners,' they told me. They condemned my house—gave me some money for what they said it was worth. And now they're going to clear it away to make a park. The park will have a nice big monument in the center—a monument to one of their own."

"Well, at least they paid you for the house," said Jonathan. He thought a moment and asked, "Weren't you satisfied?"

She gave him a sidewise look. "If I was satisfied, they wouldn't have needed a policeman to push the deal, now would they? And the money they paid me? That was taken from my neighbors. Who'll compensate them? The Lords won't pay 'em!"

Jonathan shook his head in bewilderment. "You said that it was all part of a master plan?"

"Ha! A master plan!" the woman said sarcastically. "That's a plan that belongs to whoever has political power. If I spent my life in politics, then I'd be able to impose my plans on everyone else. Then I could steal houses instead of building them. It's so much easier!"

"But surely you need a plan in order to have a wisely built town?" said Jonathan hopefully. He tried to find a logical explanation for the woman's plight. "Shouldn't you trust the Council to come up with such a plan?"

She waved her hand at the row houses. "Go see for yourself. The worst plans are the few that they actually complete—shoddy, costly, and ugly."

Turning to face Jonathan, she looked him straight in the eye. "Think of this, they built a sports stadium where nine of every ten spectators can't see the field of play. Because of their shoddy work, it cost twice as much to repair as it cost to build in the first place! And their great meeting hall is only available to visitors, not for the taxpayers who paid for it. Who did the planning? The Lords. They get their names emblazoned in stone and their friends get fat contracts."

Jabbing a finger into Jonathan's chest, she declared, "Only foolish plans have to be forced on people. Force never earned my trust!" Fuming, she glared back at her house. "They haven't heard the last from me!"

CHAPTER 8

TWO ZOOS

ontinuing on his way, Jonathan puzzled over the rules of this troubled island. Surely the people wouldn't live with laws that made them so unhappy? There must be a good reason. The land looked so green and the air was so soft and warm—this should be paradise. Jonathan relaxed into his stride as he passed through the town.

He reached a stretch of road with formidable iron fences lining both sides. Behind the fence on his right stood strange animals of many sizes and shapes—tigers, zebras, monkeys—too many to count. Behind the other fence on the left paced dozens of men and women, all wearing black-and-white-striped shirts and pants. The two groups facing each other across the road looked bizarre. Spotting a man wearing a black uniform and twirling a billy club, Jonathan approached the guard as he marched between the locked gates.

Jonathan asked politely, "What are these fences for?"

Keeping a steady rhythm with his feet and club, the guard proudly replied, "One encloses our animal zoo."

"Oh," said Jonathan, staring at a group of furry animals with prehensile tails leaping from the walls of their cage.

The guard, accustomed to giving tours to the local children, continued to lecture. "See the excellent variety of animals over there?" He gestured toward the right side of the road. "They're brought to us from all over the world. The fence keeps the animals safely in place where people can study them. Can't have strange animals wandering around and harming society, you know."

"Wow!" exclaimed Jonathan. "It must have cost you a fortune to bring animals from all over the world and to provide for them here."

The guard smiled at Jonathan, and shook his head slightly. "Oh, I don't pay for the zoo myself. Everyone on Corrumpo pays a zoo tax."

"Everyone?" asked Jonathan, self-consciously feeling the bottom of his empty pockets.

"Well, some folks try to avoid their responsibilities. These reluctant citizens say they have no interest in a zoo. Others refuse because they believe animals should be studied in their natural habitat."

The guard turned to face the fence on the left of the road, rapping the heavy iron gate with his billy. "When citizens refuse to pay the zoo tax, we place them here, safely behind these bars. Such strange people can then be studied. They, too, are prevented from wandering around and harming society."

Jonathan's head began to spin from disbelief. Comparing the two groups behind the fences, he wondered if he would pay for the maintenance of this guard and two zoos. He gripped the iron bars and scrutinized the proud faces of the inmates in striped clothing. Then he studied the haughty expression on the face of the guard who continued to pace back and forth, twirling his club.

That same old yellow cat was weaving in and out of the bars of the zoo, always on the prowl for a meal. The guard pounded a bar loudly with his stick and the cat scampered behind Jonathan's legs. He then sat down to lick his forepaw and to scratch the fleas behind his torn ear.

"I'll bet you love mice, don't you, cat? Lots of mice," said Jonathan. Patting him on the head, Jonathan christened his new companion saying, "How about 'Mices'? Well, Mices, you've been on both sides of the fence. On which side of the bars are those of greater harm?"

CHAPTER 9

MAKING MONEY

In the company of Mices, Jonathan pressed on. The buildings grew larger and more people filled the street. Sidewalks made walking easier, even for the ones on their knees. As he passed a large brick building, he heard the roar of machinery coming from above. The rapid clickety-clack sounded like a printing press. "Maybe it's the town newspaper," said Jonathan aloud, as if expecting a reply from the cat. "Good! Then I can read all about this island."

Hastily he rounded the corner looking for an entrance and nearly bumped into a smartly-dressed couple walking arm-in-arm along the cobblestone street. "Excuse me," apologized Jonathan, "is this where they print the town newspaper?"

The lady smiled and the gentleman corrected Jonathan. "I'm afraid you're mistaken, young man. This is the Official Bureau of Money Creation, not the newspaper."

"Oh," said Jonathan in disappointment. "I was hoping to find a printer of some importance."

"Cheer up," said the man. "There is no printer of greater importance than this bureau. Isn't that right dear?" The man patted the woman's gloved hand.

"Yes, that's true," said the woman with a giggle. "The Bureau brings lots of happiness with the money it prints."

"That sounds wonderful!" said Jonathan excitedly. "Money would sure make me happy right now. If I could print some money then..."

"Oh, no!" said the man in disapproval. He shook a finger in Jonathan's face. "That's out of the question."

"Of course," said the woman in agreement. "Money printers who are not appointed by the Council of Lords are branded 'counterfeiters' and thrown behind bars. We don't tolerate scoundrels."

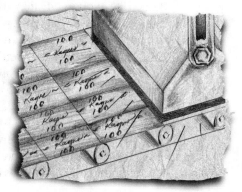

The man nodded vigorously. "When counterfeiters print their fake money and spend it, too much money circulates. Prices soar; wages, savings, and pensions become worthless. It's pure thievery!"

Jonathan frowned. What had

he missed? "I thought you said that printing lots of money makes people happy."

"Oh, yes, that's true," replied the woman. "Provided..."

"...that it's official money printing," the man interjected before she could finish. The couple knew each other so well that they finished each other's sentences. The man pulled a large leather wallet from his coat pocket and took out a piece of paper to show Jonathan. Pointing to an official seal of the Council of Lords, he noted, "See here. This says 'legal tender,' and that makes it official money."

"The printing of official money is called 'monetary policy,'" she proceeded, as though reciting from a memorized school text. "Monetary policy is all part of a master plan."

Putting his wallet away, the man added, "If it's official, then those who issue this 'legal tender' are not thieves."

"Certainly not!" said she. "The Council of Lords spends this legal tender on our behalf."

"Yes, and they are very generous," he said with a wink. "They spend that official money on projects for their loyal subjects—especially those who help them get elected."

"One more question, if you don't mind," continued Jonathan. "You said that when counterfeit money is everywhere, prices soar and wages, savings, and pensions become worthless. Doesn't this also happen with that legal tender stuff?"

The couple looked at each other gleefully. The gentlemen said, "Well, prices do rise, but we're always happy when the Lords have more money to spend on us. There are so many needs of the employed, the unemployed, the exceptional, the unexceptional, the young, the unyoung, the poor, and the unpoor."

The woman added, "The Lords research the roots of our pricing problems scrupulously. They've identified bad luck and poor weather as the chief causes. The whims of nature cause rising prices and a declining standard of living—especially in our woodlands and farmlands."

"Indeed!" exclaimed her escort. "Our island is besieged by cataclysms that ruin our economy with high prices. Surely the high prices of lumber and food will mean our downfall one day."

"And low prices," she cried. "Outsiders, with their dog-eat-dog competition, are always trying to sell us candles and coats at ruinously low prices. Our wise Council of Lords deals severely with those monsters as well." Turning to her companion she tugged impatiently at his sleeve.

"Quite right," he told her. "I hope you will excuse us, young man. We have an engagement with our investment banker. Must catch the boom in land and precious metals. Come, dear." The gentleman tipped his hat, the lady bowed politely, and both wished Jonathan a cheerful farewell.

CHAPTER 10

THE DREAM MACHINE

How would Jonathan ever get home? He was a hearty, honest lad, willing to do any kind of work. Perhaps he might find a job with a ship's crew. Surely an island had to have a harbor and ships. As he pondered the problem, a thin man struggled to load a bulky machine onto a big, horse-drawn wagon. He wore an eye-catching red suit and a stylish hat with a large feather stuck in the band. Catching sight of Jonathan, the man hollered, "Hey, kid, I'll pay you five kayns to help me load."

"Kayns?" repeated Jonathan curiously.

"Money, paper payola. Ya want it or not?"

"Sure," said Jonathan, having no better idea of what to do. It wasn't work on a ship, but he needed to earn his keep. Besides, the man looked shrewd and could offer some advice. After much pushing and shoving, they managed to heave the unwieldy machine on board. Wiping his brow, Jonathan stood back panting and looked at the object of his labor. The machine was large with beautiful designs painted all over. On the top was a large horn, such as the one Jonathan had once seen on a hand-cranked phonograph back home.

"Such beautiful colors," said Jonathan, feeling dizzy while staring at the intricate, pulsating patterns. "And what's that big horn on top?"

"Come around front and see for yourself." So Jonathan climbed up on the wagon and read the sign painted with elegant gold letters: "GOLLY GOMPER'S DREAM MACHINE!"

"A dream machine?" repeated Jonathan. "You mean it makes dreams come true?"

"It sure does," said the sharp-faced man. He twisted out the last screw and removed a panel in back of the machine. Inside were the works of a simple phonograph. Instead of a hand crank, it had a spring with a wind-up key. A switch turned the turntable on.

"There's nothing but an old music box in there!" declared Jonathan.

"What'd you expect," said the man, "a fairy godmother?"

"I don't know. I thought it would be a little, uh, mysterious. After all, it takes something special to make people's dreams come true."

A sly grin spread across the man's thin face and he gave Jonathan a long, hard look. "Words, my curious friend. It just takes words to make some dreams come true. The problem is you never know just who will get the dream when you wish for something."

Seeing Jonathan's puzzled expression, the man reached into his pocket and produced a crisp white, tiny business card. He introduced himself in his staccato nasal twang, "Tanstaafl's the name. P.T. Tanstaafl." Just then he noticed that he had given Jonathan the wrong card, one that read "G. Gomper" instead. He snatched it back. "Excuse me, son, that's yesterday's card."

Shuffling through his wallet he found another card of a slightly different size and color presenting today's name. He then pulled out a poster with elegant gold lettering that he pasted over the original name on his sign. It now read, "DR. TANSTAAFL'S DREAM MACHINE."

The man explained smoothly, "People have their dreams, right? It's just that they don't know how to make dreams come true, right?" Dr. Tanstaafl nodded his head every time he said "Right?". Jonathan began nodding dumbly in unison.

"So you pay money, turn the key, and this old box plays a certain subtle instruction over and over again, right?" Tanstaafl nodded again, Jonathan followed with a bob. "It's always the same message and there are always plenty of dreamers who love to hear it, right?"

"What's the message, Mr. Tanstaafl?" asked Jonathan, suddenly conscious of his head bobbing up and down.

The man corrected Jonathan, "Please! *Doctor* Tanstaafl. As I was saying, the Dream Machine tells people to think of whatever they would like to have, and..." The man glanced around to see if anyone else was listening. "Then it explains to the dreamers what to do—in a very persuasive manner, right?"

"You mean it hypnotizes them?" asked Jonathan, his eyes widening.

"Oh no, no, no, no, no!" objected the man. "It tells them that they are good people and that what they wish for is a good thing, right? It's so good that they should demand it, right!"

"Is that all?" Jonathan said in awe.

"That's all."

After a moment's hesitation, Jonathan asked, "So what do these dreamers demand?"

The man pulled out an oil can and proceeded to oil the gears inside. "Well, it depends a lot on where I put this machine. I frequently put it in front of a factory like this one—Bastiat Builders." He jerked a thumb in the direction of a squat two-story building across the street. "And sometimes I set up by the Palace of Lords. Around here, people always want more money. More money is a good thing, ya know, 'cuz prices are always going up and people always need more, right?"

"So I've heard," said Jonathan, rolling his eyes in sympathy. "Do they get it?"

The man pulled back and wiped his hands on a rag. "Some do—just like that!" he said with a snap of his fingers. "The dreamers stormed down to the Palace and demanded laws that would force the factory to give them a three-fold increase in pay and benefits."

"What benefits?" said Jonathan.

"Like security. More security's a good thing, right? So the dreamers demanded laws that would force factories to buy insurance for them. Insurance for sickness. Insurance for unemployment. Insurance for death, right?"

"That sounds great!" exclaimed Jonathan. "Those dreamers must have been very happy." He turned to look back at the factory and noticed that there didn't seem to be much going on. Faded paint made the buildings look tired and no lights shined from the dirty, broken windows. Pieces of shattered glass lay scattered over the sidewalk.

The man finished his oiling, replaced the back panel and tightened the screws back into place. With a final wipe of his rag over the polished surface of the box, he bounced out of the cart and went to check the harness. Jonathan jumped down and turned to the man repeating, "I said they must have been very happy—I mean to get all that money and security. And grateful, too. Did they give you a medal or a banquet to celebrate?"

"Nothing of the sort," said Dr. Tanstaafl curtly. "I nearly got tarred and feathered. They almost destroyed my delicate Dream Machine last night with rocks, bricks, and just about anything else they could throw. You see, their factory closed yesterday and the workers blamed me."

"Why'd the factory close?"

"It seems the factory couldn't earn enough to pay the workers' raises and benefits. Now they've got to retool and try making something else."

"But, then," said Jonathan, "that means the dreams didn't come true after all. If the factory closed, then nobody gets paid. And nobody gets security, either. Nobody gets anything! Why, you're just a swindler. You said that the Dream Machine..."

"Hold on there, chap! The dreams came true. What I said was," stressed the man slowly, "that you never know just who will get the dream when you wish for something. It so happens that every time an old factory closes here on the isle of Corrumpo, that very dream comes true across the waters on the Isle of Nie. A new factory recently opened there, just a week's sail from here. Plenty of new jobs and security over there. As for me, well, I collect my money from the machine no matter what happens."

Jonathan thought hard about the news of Nie, realizing that there was another island, one more prosperous than this one. "Where's this Isle of Nie?" he asked.

"Far east over the horizon. The people of Nie have a factory just like this. When factory costs rose here, the factories over there got a lot more orders. They understand that having more customers is the best way of getting more of everything—pay and security. The workers on Corrumpo can't just demand more from the customers. There ain't no such thing as a free lunch, ya know. Everything has a cost."

Dr. Tanstaafl chuckled as he tied the machine down with straps. He paid Jonathan for his help then climbed onto the driver's seat and shook out the reins. Jonathan looked at the money he had been given and suddenly worried that it was soon going to be worthless. It was the same legal tender the couple had shown him in front of the Official Bureau of Money Creation. "Hey, Dr. Tanstaafl, wait!"

"Yeah?"

"Could you pay me with some other kind of money? I mean, something that's not going to lose value?"

"It's legal tender, pal. Ya gotta take it. Do you think I'd use this stuff if I had a choice? Just spend it quickly!" The man yelled at his horse and he was off.

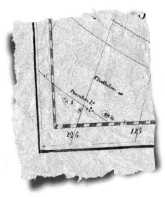

CHAPTER 11

POWER SALE

husky, jolly woman bore down on Jonathan as he stood wondering where to go next. Without hesitation, she grabbed his right hand and began to pump it vigorously. "How do you do? Isn't it a fine day?" she said at rapid-fire speed, still working his hand with her meaty arm. "I'm Lady Bess Tweed, your friendly neighborhood representative on the Council of Lords, and I would be most grateful to have your contribution and your vote for my reelection to office and there you have it, that is the pressing situation for our fine community."

"Really?" said Jonathan. The speed and force of her speech knocked Jonathan back a step. He had never met a person who could say so many words in one breath.

"Oh yes," continued Lady Tweed, barely listening to his reply, "and I am willing to pay you well, oh yes, I am willing to pay you, you can't ask for a better deal, and how about that?"

"Pay me for a contribution and a vote?" asked Jonathan with a puzzled look.

"Of course, I can't give you cash—that would be illegal, a bribe— say no more, say no more!" said Lady Tweed, winking slyly at him and poking him in the ribs with her elbow. She continued, "But I can give you something just as good as cash and worth many times the amount of your contribution to me. It's as easy as priming a pump. A few bills in my palm right now and you can expect a gusher of goodies later. That's what I'll do and how about that?"

"That would be nice," replied Jonathan, who could see she wasn't listening to him anyway.

"What's your occupation? I can arrange assistance—loans or licenses or subsidies or tax breaks. I can ruin your competitors with rules and regulations and inspections and fees. So you can see, there is no better investment in the world than a well-placed politician. Perhaps you'd like a new road or a park built in your neighborhood or maybe a large building or..."

"Wait!" shouted Jonathan, trying to stop the torrent of words. "How can you give me more than I give you? Are you so very rich and generous?"

"Me rich? Saints and bullfrogs, no!" retorted Lady Tweed. "I'm not rich. Well, not that I will admit. Generous? You could say so, but I don't plan to pay with my own money. Of course, you see, I'm in charge of the official treasury. And, to be sure, I can be very generous with those funds, to the right people..." She grinned, winked twice and nudged him again in the ribs. "Say no more, say no more!"

Jonathan still did not understand what she meant. "But, if you buy my contribution and my vote, isn't that sort of like, well, the same as bribery?"

Lady Tweed gave him a shrewd look. "I'll be blunt with you, my dear friend." She draped one arm over his shoulder and pulled him uncomfortably tight against her side. "It is bribery. But it's legal when a politician uses money from other people rather than from his or her own pocket. Likewise, it is illegal for you to give me cash for specific favors, unless you call it a 'campaign contribution.' Then everything is okay. You can buy a hundred copies of my memoirs and not read a single one. Feel uncomfortable giving cash to me directly? Just ask a friend or a relative or an associate to offer permanent loans, stock options, or benefits to me or my kin—now or later." She paused expectantly. "Now, do you understand?"

Jonathan shook his head, "I still don't see the difference. I mean, bribing people for votes and favors is still bribery no matter who they are or whose money it is. The label makes no difference if the deed is the same."

Lady Tweed smiled indulgently, "My dear, dear friend, you've got to be more flexible. The label is everything." With her free hand, she gently grasped his chin and turned Jonathan's head sideways "What's your name? Did you know you've got a nice profile? You could go a long way if you ran for public office. If you're flexible, I'm sure that I could find you a nice post in my bureau after reelection. Or is there something else you want?"

Jonathan shook his head free and managed to wriggle out from under her arm. "What do you get by giving away taxpayers' money? Can you keep the money that's given to you as contributions?"

"Oh, some of it is useful for my expenses and I have a fortune promised to me should I ever retire, but mostly it buys me recognition or credibility or popularity or love or admiration or a place in history. All this and more for me and my progeny!" Lady Tweed chuckled softly. "Votes are power and there is nothing I enjoy more than having influence over the life, liberty, and property of every person on this island. Can you imagine how many people come to me—*me*—for big and little favors? Every tax and regulation presents an opportunity for me to grant a special exception. Every problem, big or little, gives me more influence. I award free lunches and free rides to whomever I choose. Ever since I was a child I dreamed of such importance. You, too, can share the glory!"

Jonathan tried to free his hand. But Lady Tweed kept him firmly in her eel-like grip. "Sure," said Jonathan, "you and your friends have a great deal, but don't other people get upset when you use their money to buy votes, favors, and power?"

"Certainly," she said, lifting up her plump, double-chinned jaw proudly. "And I hear their concerns. So I've become the champion of reform." Finally releasing Jonathan's hand, Lady Tweed thrust her large, bejeweled fist into the air. "For years I've drafted new rules to take the money out of politics. I always say that campaign money causes a crisis of major proportion. And I have won a fair share of votes with promises for reform." She paused to smirk and continued, "Fortunately for me, I always know a way around my rules so long as there are valuable favors to sell." She winked and nudged again, "Know what I mean, know what I mean?"

Lady Tweed eyed Jonathan critically, taking in his tattered appearance. "No one pays you a penny for favors because you, as yet, have no favors to sell. Don't you see? But, with your innocent looks—and the right backing from me, you could go far. Hmm...a new set of clothes, elevated shoes, a stylish haircut, and the proper fiancée. Yes, I could definitely triple the beginner's vote tally for you. Then, after ten or twenty years of careful guidance—well, there's no limit to the possibilities! Look me up at the Palace of Lords and I'll see what I can do." Lady Tweed spotted a group of workers that had gathered across the street, looking forlornly at the shuttered factory. She abruptly lost interest in Jonathan and marched swiftly away, searching for fresh prey.

"Spending other people's money sounds like trouble," mumbled Jonathan.

With ears keenly tuned to any sound of disagreement, Lady Tweed stopped and turned quickly, "Did you say 'trouble'? Ha! It really is like taking candy from a baby. What the people don't give to me out of duty, I borrow from them. You see, I'll be long gone and fondly remembered when their yet-unborn-babies get the bill. What's your name, boy?"

"Uh, Jonathan Gullible, ma'am."

Lady Tweed's face turned hard and cold. "I'll remember you, Jonathan Gullible. If you're not with me, you're against me. I reward friends and punish enemies. You can't stand in the middle, understand me? There you have it, that is the pressing situation for our fine community. Say no more!" In a blink, her face snapped back into a broad, beaming smile. Then she vanished down the street.

CHAPTER 12

HELTER SHELTER

The streets grew quieter as Jonathan trudged down yet another row of drab houses. He noticed a group of poorly dressed people gathered in front of three tall buildings labeled BLOCK A, BLOCK B, and BLOCK C. BLOCK A was vacant and in appalling condition—the masonry crumbling, the windows broken, and any remaining panes filthy with grime. Next door at BLOCK B, people huddled on the front steps. Jonathan heard loud voices coming from inside and the sounds of lively activity from all three floors. Laundry hung untidily from sticks that protruded from every available window and balcony. It burst at the seams with tenants.

Across the street, stood BLOCK C, immaculately maintained and, like BLOCK A, empty of people. Its scrubbed windows sparkled in the sunlight; stucco walls were smooth and clean.

As he gazed at the three buildings, Jonathan felt a light tap on his shoulder. Turning, he faced a young girl with long sandy brown hair. Her light gray clothes fitted her poorly and she wasn't especially pretty at first sight, but Jonathan thought she looked alert and kind.

"Do you know of any apartments for rent?" she asked in a soft, pleasant voice.

"I'm sorry," said Jonathan. "I'm not from around here. But why don't you check those two vacant buildings?"

"It's no use," she responded softly.

"But," said Jonathan, "they look empty to me."

"They are. My family used to live over there in BLOCK A before rent control."

"What's rent control?" asked Jonathan.

"It's a law to stop landlords from raising rents."

"Why?" probed Jonathan.

"Oh, it's a silly story," she said. "Back when the Dream Machine came through our neighborhood, my dad and other tenants complained about landlords raising rents. Sure, costs were up and more people were renting, but my dad said that was no reason for us to pay more. So the tenants—or former tenants, I should say—demanded that the Council of Lords prohibit the raising of rents. The Council did just that and hired a slew of administrators, inspectors, judges, and guards to enforce the new rules."

"Were the tenants pleased?"

"At first, sure. My dad felt secure about the cost of a roof over our heads. But then the landlords stopped building new apartments and stopped fixing the old ones."

"What happened?"

"Costs kept going up—repairmen, security guards, managers, utilities, taxes, and the like—but the landlords couldn't raise the rents to pay for it all. So they figured 'Why build and fix just to lose money?'"

"Taxes went up, too?" asked Jonathan.

"Sure, to pay for enforcing rent control. Budgets and staff had to grow," said the girl. "The Council passed rent control, but never tax control. Well, when repairs and upkeep stopped, everyone started to hate the landlords."

"They weren't always hated?"

"Nah, before rent control, we had lots of apartments to choose from. Landlords had to be nice to get us to move in and stay. Most landlords acted friendly and made things attractive. If there were any nasty landlords, word got around fast and people avoided them like the rats they were. Nice landlords attracted steady tenants while nasty ones suffered a plague of vacancies."

"What changed?"

"After rent control everyone got nasty," she said with a look of despair. "The worst prospered the most." She sat down on the curb to scratch Mices behind the ears. Mices rolled over and began to purr.

Aware of Jonathan staring at her, she continued confidently, "Costs went up, but not the rents. Even the nicest landlords had to cut back on repairs. When buildings became uncomfortable or dangerous, tenants got mad and complained to the inspectors. The inspectors slapped fines on the landlords. Of course, some landlords bribed inspectors to look the other way. Finally, the owner of BLOCK A, a decent man, couldn't afford the losses or bribes anymore so he just up and left."

"Abandoned his own building?" sputtered Jonathan.

"Yeah. It happens a lot," she sighed. "Imagine walking away from something that took a lifetime to build? Well, fewer and fewer apartments were available but the number of tenants kept growing. People had to squeeze into whatever was left. Even mean landlords, like the one who holds BLOCK B, never had a vacancy again. Rumor has it that he takes payoffs under the table just to move applicants higher up the waiting list. Those with enough cash get by okay. That nasty owner makes out like a bandit."

"What about BLOCK B?" said Jonathan, wanting to be helpful. "Can you get in?"

"The waiting line is awful. When Dame Whitmore passed away you should have seen the brawl out front—everyone scratching and yelling at each other for position in line. Lady Tweed's son finally got that apartment—even though nobody remembers seeing him in line that day. My family once tried to share an apartment in BLOCK B, but the building code prohibits sharing."

"What's a building code?" asked Jonathan.

The girl frowned. "It started as a set of rules for safety. But the Lords now use it to determine lifestyle. You know, things like the right number of sinks, stoves, and toilets; the right number and kind of people; the right amount of space." With a tinge of sarcasm she added, "So we ended up in the street where nothing meets the code—no sinks, stoves, or toilets, no privacy, and far too much space."

Jonathan grew depressed thinking about her plight. Then he remembered the third building—brand new and vacant. It was the obvious solution to her problems. "Why don't you move into BLOCK C, right there across the street?"

She laughed bitterly. "That would be a violation of the zoning rules."

"Zoning rules?" he repeated. Leaning back on the sidewalk where he sat, Jonathan shook his head, incredulous.

"Those are rules about location. Zoning works like this," she said picking up a stick to sketch a little map in the dirt. "The Council draws lines on a map of the town. People are allowed to sleep on one side of the line at night, but they must work on the other side during the day. BLOCK B is on the sleep side of the line and BLOCK C is on the work side. Usually work buildings are located across town from sleep buildings so that everyone needs to travel a lot every morning and evening. They say the long distances are good for exercise and carriage sales."

Jonathan stared in bewilderment. A packed apartment building standing between two empty buildings and a street full of indigents. Sympathetically he asked, "What are you going to do?"

"We take one day at a time. My dad wants me to go with him to the gala 'Thumbs Up Party' that Lady Tweed is putting on for the homeless tomorrow. She promises to lift our spirits with games and a free lunch."

"How generous," remarked Jonathan drily, recalling his conversation with Lady Tweed. "Maybe she'd let you live in her house until you find something of your own."

"Dad actually had the nerve to ask her that once, especially since Tweed led the Council in putting through rent controls. Lady Tweed declared, 'But that would be charity! Charity is demeaning!' She explained to him that it is far more respectable to require taxpayers give us housing. She told him to be patient and that she'd make arrangements with the Council."

The young woman smiled at Jonathan and asked, "By the way, they call me Alisa. Do you want to join us at Tweed's free lunch tomorrow afternoon?"

Jonathan blushed. Maybe he could learn to enjoy this island. "Sure, I'd love to come along. By the way, I'm Jonathan."

Alisa jumped up, smiling. "Then, Jonathan, we meet here tomorrow—same time. Bring your cat."

CHAPTER 13

ESCALATING CRIMES

appy to find a new friend, Jonathan wandered off in a daze. With a start, he realized that he had better pay closer attention to his surroundings or he would not be able to return the next day.

He happened across a policeman, not much older than himself, who was sitting on a bench reading a newspaper. Jonathan tensed at the sight of the crisp black uniform and shiny gun. But the youthful, open expression on the policeman's faced made Jonathan relax. The policeman was totally engrossed in a newspaper and Jonathan glanced over at the headlines: "LORDS APPROVE DEATH PENALTY FOR OUTLAW BARBERS!"

"The death penalty for barbers?" exclaimed Jonathan in surprise.

The policeman glanced up at Jonathan.

"Excuse me," said Jonathan. "I didn't mean to bother you, but I couldn't help seeing the headline. Is that a misprint about the punishment?"

"Well, let's see." The officer read aloud, "'The Council of Lords has just authorized the death penalty for anyone found to be cutting hair without a license.' Hmm, no misprint. What's so unusual about that?"

"Isn't that quite severe for such a minor offense?" asked Jonathan cautiously.

"Hardly," replied the policeman. "The death penalty is the ultimate threat behind all laws—no matter how minor the offense."

Jonathan's eyes widened. "Surely you wouldn't put someone to death for cutting hair without a license?"

"Of course we would," said the policeman, patting his gun for emphasis. "Though it seldom comes to that."

"Why?"

"Well, every crime escalates in severity. That means the penalties increase the more one resists. For example, if someone wishes to cut hair without a license, then a fine will be levied. If he or she refuses to pay the fine or continues to cut hair, then the outlaw barber will be arrested and put behind bars. And," said the man in a sober tone, "resisting arrest subjects a criminal to severe penalties." His face darkened with a frown. "The outlaw may even be shot. The greater the resistance, the greater the force used against him."

Such a grim discussion depressed Jonathan. "So the ultimate threat behind every law really is death? Surely the authorities would reserve the death penalty for only the most brutal, criminal acts—violent acts like murder and rape!"

"No," said the police officer. "The law regulates the whole range of personal and commercial life. Hundreds of occupational guilds protect their members with licenses like these. Carpenters, doctors, plumbers, accountants, bricklayers, and lawyers—you name it, they all hate interlopers."

"How do licenses protect them?" asked Jonathan.

"The number of licenses is restricted to the few who pass the rituals of guild membership. This eliminates the unfair competition of intruders with peculiar new ideas, overzealous enthusiasm, backbreaking efficiency, or cutthroat prices. Such unscrupulous anti-competitive competition threatens the traditions of our most esteemed professions."

Jonathan still didn't understand. "Does licensing protect customers?"

"Oh, yes. Says so right here." The policeman turned back to the newspaper reading, "'Licenses give monopolies to guilds so that they can protect customers from unwise decisions and too many choices.'" Tapping his chest proudly, the policeman added, "And I enforce the monopolies."

"Monopolies are good?" probed Jonathan.

The policeman frowned, lowering his newspaper. "I don't know, really. I just follow orders. Sometimes I enforce monopolies and sometimes I'm told to break monopolies."

"So which is right?"

The policeman shrugged. "That's not for me to figure out. The Council of Lords decides and tells me where to point my gun."

Seeing Jonathan's look of alarm, the policeman tried to reassure him. "Don't worry. We seldom carry out the death penalty itself. Few dare to resist since we are diligent at teaching obedience to the Council. It's so rarely mentioned that my chief, Officer Stuart, calls it 'The Invisible Gun'."

"Have you ever used yours?" said Jonathan, eyeing the pistol nervously.

"Against an outlaw?" asked the policeman. With a practiced motion, he pulled the revolver smoothly from its leather holster and stroked the cold-steel muzzle. "Only once." He opened the chamber, looked down the barrel, snapped it shut, and admired the gun. "Some of the very best technology on the island here. The Council spares no effort to give us the finest tools for our noble mission. Yes, this gun and I are sworn to protect the life, liberty, and property of everyone on the island."

"When did you use it?" asked Jonathan.

"Strange you should ask," he said, suddenly downcast. "A whole year on duty and I never had to use it until just this morning. Some old woman went crazy and started threatening a demolition crew with a stick. Said something about taking back her 'own' house. Ha! What a selfish notion."

Jonathan's heart skipped a beat. He remembered the elegant white house and the dignified woman who claimed ownership. The policeman continued, "I tried to persuade her to give up. The paperwork was all in order—the house had been condemned to make way for the Lady Tweed People's Park."

Jonathan could barely speak. "What happened?"

"I tried to reason with her. Told her she could probably get off with a light sentence if she came along with me peacefully. But then she threatened me, told me to get off her property! Well, it was a clear case of resisting arrest. Imagine the nerve of that woman!"

"Yes," sighed Jonathan. "What nerve."

The conversation died. The policeman read quietly while Jonathan stood silent, nudging a stone with his foot. Summoning his nerve, Jonathan asked, "Can anyone buy a gun like yours?"

Turning a page of the newspaper, the policeman replied, "Not on your life. Someone might get hurt."

CHAPTER 14

BOOK BATTLES

ctivity on the streets increased as Jonathan continued toward the center of town. Mices followed him at a distance. Here was a cat with a purpose—to catch every rat or uncover any food possible. He covered three times the distance that Jonathan did, exploring back alleys, garbage cans, and crawlspaces. The cat's yellow hair grew dusty and shabby, despite his constant grooming.

Well-dressed individuals with preoccupied expressions marched or knee-shuffled briskly along the sidewalks. Crossing a large open square, Jonathan encountered an elderly man and a young woman having a vicious shouting match. They cursed and hollered, waving their arms violently in the air. Jonathan joined a small gathering of bystanders to see what the fight was all about.

Just as the police arrived to pull them apart, Jonathan tapped the shoulder of a frail old woman leaning on a cane and inquired, "Why are they so angry with each other?"

The woman had deep wrinkles and creases across her face and hands. She regarded young Jonathan carefully before replying in a thin quavering voice. "These two rowdies have been screaming at each other for years about the books in the Council library. The man always complains that many of the books are full of trashy sex and immorality. He wants those books taken out and burned, while she reacts by calling him a 'pompous puritan'."

"She wants to read those books?" asked Jonathan.

"Well, not exactly," snickered a tall man, kneeling nearby. A little girl stood at his side. "She complains about different books. She claims that many of the books in the library have a sexist and racist bias."

"Daddy, Daddy, what is 'bias'?" pleaded the little girl while tugging at his shoulder.

"Later, dear. As I was saying," continued the man, "the woman demands that those sexist and racist books be thrown out and that the library purchase her list of books instead."

By now the police had handcuffed both of the fighters and were dragging them down the street. Jonathan shook his head and sighed. "I suppose the police arrested them for this brawl?"

"Not at all," laughed the old woman. "The police arrested both of them for refusing to pay the library tax. According to the law, everyone must pay for all the books whether they like them or not."

"Really?" said Jonathan. "Why don't the police just let the people keep their money and let them pay for what they like?"

"But then my daughter couldn't afford to go to a library," said the kneeling man. He peeled the wrapping from a big red-and-white spiral candy cane and handed it to his daughter.

"Hold on, mister," said the old woman as she shot a look of disapproval at the candy. "Isn't food for your daughter's mind just as important as food for her stomach?"

"What are you getting at?" responded the man defensively. His daughter had already managed to smear the candy across her dress.

The woman replied firmly, "Long ago we had a great variety of subscription libraries—known then as 'scriptlibs.' It cost a small membership fee every year and no one complained because they only paid for the scriptlibs that they liked. Scriptlibs even competed for members, trying to have the best books and staff, the most convenient hours and locations. Some even went door-to-door to pick up and deliver books. People paid for their choices because library membership was important to them." She added, "A higher priority than candy!"

Turning directly to Jonathan, she explained, "Then the Council of Lords decided that a library was too important to be left to individual caprice. At taxpayer expense, the Council created the GLIB, a large government library. The GLIB became popular because it was free— people never had to pay to use the books. To do the work of each scriptlib librarian, the Council hired three GLIB librarians at top salaries. Shortly thereafter, the scriptlibs closed."

"The Lords provided a library for free?" repeated Jonathan. "But I thought you said that everyone had to pay a library tax?"

"That's true. But it's customary to call Council facilities 'free' even though people are forced to pay. It's much more civilized," she said in a voice heavy with irony.

The tall man objected strenuously, "Subscription libraries? I never heard of such a thing!"

"Of course not," retorted the old woman. "The GLIB has been around so long that you can't imagine anything else."

"Now, hold on there!" cried the man, hobbling forward on his knees. "Are you criticizing the library tax? If the Lords provide a valued service, then people must pay."

"How valued is it if they have to use force?" said the old woman. She stood glaring eye-to-eye at the tall man on his knees.

"Not everyone knows what's good for them! And some can't afford it," declared the man. "Intelligent people know that free books build a free society. And taxes spread the burden so that everyone has to pay their fair share. Otherwise freeloaders might ride on the backs of others!"

"There are more freeloaders now than ever," replied the old woman. "Frequent users and those with tax exemptions ride on the backs of everyone else. How fair is that? Who do you think has more influence with the Council of Lords? A well-connected supporter or some poor guy who gets off work after GLIB closing hours?"

Pushing his little girl behind him and edging forward, the man retorted hotly, "Just what kind of a library choice do you want? Do you want to choose a subscription library that may be biased against some group in society?"

"You can't avoid bias!" the woman screamed, leaning close to his face. "Do you want buffoons in the Council to choose your bias for you?"

"Who's the buffoon?" countered the man, shoving the old woman slightly off balance. "If you don't like it, then why don't you just leave Corrumpo!"

"You insolent rascal!" replied the woman, popping him on the head with her cane. "I've been paying for your GLIB since before you were born!"

By now the two were yelling at each other, the little girl was crying, and someone shuffled off to summon the police—again. Jonathan edged past them and fled the square for the peace and quiet of the nearby GLIB.

CHAPTER 15

NOTHING TO IT

he GLIB structure stood two stories high with an impressive stone façade. A well-dressed crowd clustered at the entrance, waiting to enter. They pretended not to notice the mounting quarrel that flared behind them in the square. As Jonathan joined the group, he read with interest the heavy bronze letters above the doorway, "LADY BESS TWEED PEOPLE'S LIBRARY."

Visitors far in back of the crowd craned to look over those standing in front. They exclaimed aloud at what they saw. "Marvelous," whispered some. "Stunning," said others. Try as he might, Jonathan couldn't see what caught their attention.

Deft and slim, Jonathan squeezed around the crowd and approached a librarian's desk inside the entrance. "What does this group find so marvelous and stunning?" he asked of the man sitting behind the desk.

"Shhhh!" admonished the librarian sternly. "Please lower your voice." The man tapped the corners of a pile of note cards and laid them down neatly in front of him. He bent forward and looked at Jonathan over his half-framed glasses. "These are members of the Council's Commission on the Arts. They have just opened an exhibit of the latest acquisition for our collection of fine art."

"How nice," whispered Jonathan. Stretching his neck to catch a glimpse, he said, "I love good art, but where is it? It must be very small."

"That depends," sniffed the librarian. "Some would say it is very expansive. That's the beauty of this piece. It's titled 'Void in Flight'."

"But I don't see anything," said Jonathan, frowning as he scanned the great white space above the entrance.

"That's the point. Impressive, isn't it?" The librarian stared at the space with a vacant, dreamy expression. "Nothing captures the full essence of the spirit of human struggle for that exalted sense of awareness that one only feels when contrasting the fuller warmth of the finer hues with the tactile awareness of our inner nature. Nothing allows everyone to fully experience the best of the collective imagination."

Befuddled, Jonathan shook his head and asked in puzzlement, "So it's really nothing? How can *nothing* be art?"

"That's precisely what makes it the most egalitarian expression of art. The Council's Commission on the Arts holds a tastefully executed lottery to make the selection," said the librarian.

"A lottery to select art?" asked Jonathan in astonishment. "Why a lottery?"

"In more backward days an appointed Board of Fine Art made the selections," replied the man. "At first, critics accused the Board of favoring their own tastes. They censored art that they disliked. Since the ordinary citizen paid for the preferences of the Board through taxes, people objected to the elitism."

"What about trying a different Board?" suggested Jonathan.

"Oh, yes, we tried that many times. But people sitting on the Board could never agree with those who were not on the Board. So they finally scrapped the whole Board idea—replaced it with our new Commission and lottery. Everyone agreed that a lottery was the only objectively subjective method. Anyone could enter the competition—and nearly everyone did! The Council of Lords made the prize as generous as possible and any piece qualified. 'Void in Flight' won the drawing just this morning."

Jonathan interjected, "But why not let everyone buy their own art instead of taxing them to buy a lottery selection? Then everyone could pick what they like."

"What!" the librarian exclaimed. "Some selfish individuals might not buy anything and others might have bad taste. No, indeed, the Lords must show their support for the arts!" Concentrating on "Void in Flight," the librarian crossed his arms and a vague expression covered his face. "Nice selection, don't you agree? Emptiness has the advantage of keeping the library entrance uncluttered while simultaneously preserving the environment. Moreover," he continued happily, "no one can object to the artistic quality or to the aesthetic style of this masterpiece. Who could possibly be offended?"

CHAPTER 16

THE SPECIAL INTEREST CARNIVAL

he sun was setting as Jonathan returned to the steps of the library. To his delight, the town came to life after dark; people began milling about in the square. More and more people streamed toward a magnificent carnival tent standing near the GLIB.

Gawking at the lights, sights, and sounds, Jonathan wandered over to the spectacular tent. A colorful sign overhead read: "CARNIVAL OF SPECIAL INTERESTS."

A striking woman wearing a tight, garishly-colored costume sprang out of the crowd and shouted to all: "Hear ye, hear ye! For the thrill of a lifetime, step right up to the Carnival of Special Interests." She spotted Jonathan, whose eyes opened wide with surprise, and grabbed his arm. "Everyone is a winner, young man."

"What's it cost?" asked Jonathan.

"Bring in ten kayns and walk out with a fabulous prize!" she replied. The woman gestured widely to the crowd, "Hear ye, hear ye! The Carnival of Special Interests will make you rich!"

Not having enough money, Jonathan waited until the woman was busy with others and then crept around to the back of the tent. He lifted the edge of the canvas to peer inside. People sat in stands along the sides of the tent. In the middle, ushers in uniform directed participants to chairs arranged in a large circle. Ten participants stood or kneeled behind their chairs expectantly. Then, half the candles were snuffed, a drum rolled, and hidden trumpets blared a fanfare. A brilliant lamp flashed on a handsome man wearing a shiny black suit and silk top hat. He bowed low to the circle of ten.

"Good evening," said the man, flashing a gleaming white-toothed smile. "I am the Circle Master! Tonight, you fortunate ten will be the lucky winners in our remarkable game. All of you will win. All of you will leave happier than when you entered. Please be seated." With that and a swift flourish of his white-gloved hand, the Circle Master collected one kayn from each participant. No one hesitated.

Then the Circle Master smiled again and announced, "Now you will see how you are rewarded." And he suddenly dropped five kayns into the lap of one participant. The lucky recipient screamed with glee.

"You won't be the only winner," declared the Circle Master. And so it was. Ten times he went around the group, collecting one kayn from each person. After each round, he dropped five kayns into the lap of one of the participants, and each time the recipient jumped for joy.

When the shouting stopped and the participants began to file out, Jonathan ran around to the front of the tent to see if everyone was really satisfied. The woman at the entrance held the tent flap open. She stopped one of the participants as he shuffled out on his knees and asked: "Did you have fun?"

"Oh sure!" the man said, grinning happily. "It was terrific!"

"I can't wait to tell my friends," said another. "I may come back again later."

Then another excited participant added, "Yes, oh yes. Everyone won a prize of five kayns!"

Jonathan thoughtfully watched the group as they dispersed. The woman turned to the Circle Master, who waved his good-bye to the crowd, and commented quietly, "Yes, we're especially happy. We won fifty kayns and these suckers all feel happy about it! I think that next year we ought to ask the Council of Lords to pass a law that will require everyone to play!"

Just then an usher sneaked behind Jonathan and grabbed him by the collar. "Hold on there, you scamp. I saw you peeking in the back. You thought you could get a free show, did ya?"

"I'm sorry," said Jonathan, struggling to get out of the usher's grasp. "I didn't realize you had to pay just to watch. That pretty lady made it sound so interesting—and I didn't have enough money, please..."

The Circle Master scowled at Jonathan and the usher, "No money?" But the woman smiled at Jonathan's compliment. "Wait, turn him loose," she said to the usher. "He's just a kid. So you liked the show, did you?"

"Oh yes, ma'am!" said Jonathan, nodding hard.

"Well, how would you like to earn some easy money? It's either that or," her voice turned threatening, "I'll turn you in to the carnival guard."

"Oh, great," said Jonathan, uncertainly. "What do you want me to do?"

"It's simple," she smiled, all sweetness again. "Just walk around the town this evening, hand out these flyers, and tell everyone how much fun they'll have in our Carnival. Here's a kayn now and you'll earn another with each participant that comes in the door carrying one of these flyers. Now go to it and don't disappoint me."

As Jonathan slung the bag of flyers over his shoulder, she cautioned, "One more thing. At the end of the show tonight, I'll turn in a report of your earnings. First thing in the morning, you must turn over half of your pay at the town hall for your tax."

"Tax?" repeated Jonathan. "Why?"

"The Lords require a share of your wages."

Jonathan didn't like the idea. He added hopefully, "If you don't report my earnings, I might work harder. Maybe twice as hard."

"The Lords are wise to that, kid. They have spies everywhere, watching us closely. If they see us hide your earnings, it could mean big trouble—might even shut us down," said the woman. "So don't complain. We must all pay for our sins."

"Sins?" repeated Jonathan.

"Oh, yes. Taxes punish the sinful. The tobacco tax punishes smoking, the alcohol tax punishes drinking, the interest tax punishes saving, and the income tax punishes working. The ideal of the Council," chuckled the woman as she winked at the Circle Master standing at her side, "is to be healthy, sober, dependent, and idle. Now get a move on, kid!"

CHAPTER 17

UNCLE SAMTA

By the time Jonathan returned to the carnival tent, he had earned more than fifty kayns. The woman was so pleased to find someone who took work seriously that she asked him to come back the next night. Jonathan agreed to return if he could, then he left the carnival to look for a bed for the night. He had no idea what to do, so he just wandered aimlessly through the town. As he paused in the dim glow of a street lamp, a short, elderly man in a nightshirt stepped out onto the front porch of a nearby house. He squinted and peered over the rooftops of the row houses bordering the street.

Curious, Jonathan asked, "What are you looking at?"

"The roof of that house," whispered the man, pointing into the dark. "See that fat guy dressed in red, white, and blue? His bag of loot gets bigger with every house he visits."

Jonathan looked in the direction the man pointed. A vague shadowy shape scrambled over the roof of one of the houses. "Why, yes, I see him! Why don't you sound the alarm and warn the people living there?"

"Oh, I'd never do that," shuddered the man. "Uncle Samta has a vicious temper and deals harshly with anyone who gets in his way."

"You know him?" protested Jonathan. "But..."

"Shhhh! Not so loud," said the old man, holding a finger to his lips. "Uncle Samta makes extra visits to those who make too much noise. Most people pretend to sleep through this awful night—though it's impossible to ignore such an invasion of privacy."

Trying to speak softly, Jonathan leaned close to the man's ear. "I don't get it. Why does everyone close their eyes when they're being robbed?"

"People keep silent on this particular night in April," the old man explained. "Otherwise it might spoil the thrill they get on Xmas Eve when Uncle Samta returns to sprinkle some toys and trinkets in every house."

"Oh," said Jonathan, with a look of relief. "So Uncle Samta gives everything back again?"

"Hardly! But people like to imagine that he does. I try to stay awake in order to keep track of what he takes and what he returns. Kind of a hobby of mine, you might say. By my calculation, Uncle Samta keeps most for himself and a few favored households around town. But," said the old man, pounding his palm against a railing in frustration, "Uncle Samta is careful to give everyone a little bit to keep them happy. That makes everyone stay asleep the following April when he comes back again to take what he wants."

"I don't understand," said Jonathan. "Why don't people stay awake, report the thief, and keep their own belongings? Then they could buy whatever trinkets they want and give them to whomever they please."

The old man chuckled and shook his head at Jonathan's naiveté. "Uncle Samta is really everyone's childhood fantasy. Parents have always taught their children that Uncle Samta's toys and trinkets come magically out of the sky and at no cost to anyone."

Seeing Jonathan's haggard appearance the old man said, "Looks like you've had a rough day, young fella."

"I was looking for a place to spend the night," Jonathan said, shyly.

"Well, you look like a nice lad," said the man, "Why don't you stay with us. Rose and I have the whole place to ourselves."

Jonathan welcomed the old man's offer. Inside Jonathan met Rose, the old man's plump wife; she cheerily brought him a cup of hot chocolate and a plate of freshly baked cookies. After the last crumb disappeared, Jonathan stretched out on a divan that the couple had made up with some blankets and a pillow. The old man lit a long pipe and leaned back into the cushions of his rocking chair.

Their home was not large, not richly furnished, and definitely not new. But, to the tired young stranger, it was the perfect refuge. A small fire in the fireplace warmed and lit the wood paneled room. Over the mantle hung two frames, one holding a family portrait and another displaying a family tree. On the simple plank floor was a well-worn, oval rug. Settling in, Jonathan asked, "How did this April tradition start?"

"We used to have a holiday called 'Christmas,' a wonderful time of year. It was a religious holiday marked by gift-giving and merriment. Everyone enjoyed it so much that the Council of Lords decided that it was too important to be left to unbridled spontaneity and chaotic celebration. They took it over so that it could be run 'correctly.'" His sarcastic tone revealed disapproval. "First, inappropriate religious symbolism had to go. The Lords officially changed the name of the holiday to 'Xmas.' And the popular mythical gift-giver was renamed 'Uncle Samta,' with the tax collector donning the costume."

The old man paused to take a couple of deep puffs and to tamp down the tobacco. He continued, "Xmas tax forms must now be submitted in triplicate to the Bureau of Good Will. The Bureau of Good Will determines the generosity required of every taxpayer based on a formula set by the Lords. You've just witnessed the annual collection.

"Next comes the Bureau of Naughty and Nice. With the assistance of an official Accountant for Morals, everyone files a form explaining in detail good and bad behavior throughout the year. The Bureau of Naughty and Nice employs an army of clerks and investigators to examine the worthiness of those who petition to receive gifts in December.

"Finally, the Commission on Correct Taste standardizes the sizes, colors, and styles of permissible gift selections, issuing non-bid contracts to pre-selected manufacturers with the proper political affiliation. Everyone, without discrimination, receives exactly the same government-issued holiday ornaments for use in decorating their homes. On Xmas eve, the militia is called out to sing the appropriate festive songs."

By now, the weary young adventurer had fallen fast asleep. As the old man pulled up the blanket over Jonathan's shoulders, a cat's meow could be heard outside the window. Rose whispered, "Merry Xmas!"

CHAPTER 18

THE TORTOISE AND THE HARE REVISITED

onathan dreamed of the woman from the Carnival of Special Interests. She kept handing him money and then grabbing it away again. Again and again, she paid him and then proceeded to snatch it back. Suddenly Jonathan woke with a jolt, remembering that he had to report his earnings to the tax officials.

The delicious smell of freshly toasted bread filled his nose. The old man stood at the table, dishing out thick slices of toast and jam for breakfast. Jonathan noticed a sad-faced little boy sitting at the table. The old man introduced the boy as their grandson, Davy, who would be staying with them awhile.

"I remember you," chirped Davy. "Grandpa, he helped me and mama when we had to leave the farm." This news made Jonathan all the more welcome. As Jonathan bit into a thickly buttered slice of toast, the little boy fidgeted restlessly, trying to pull up his mismatched socks. "Grandma, please read me the story again," he begged.

"Which one, sweetie?" She heaped hot scrambled eggs on Jonathan's plate.

"My favorite, the one about the tortoise and the hare. The pictures are so fun," beamed Davy.

"Well, all right," said Rose, taking a book from the kitchen cabinet. She sat down next to tiny Davy and began. Once upon a time..."

"No, no, Grandma, 'a long time ago...'" interrupted the boy.

Rose laughed. "As I was saying...'a long time ago there lived a tortoise named Frank and a hare named Lysander. Both of the animals worked delivering letters to all who lived in their small village. One day Frank, whose sharp ears were far more efficient than his short legs, overheard a few of the animals praise Lysander for being so quick at his deliveries. The fleet-footed hare could deliver in a few hours what others required days to do. Incensed, Frank crawled over and butted into the conversation.

"'Hare,' said Frank almost as slowly as he walked, 'in one week, I'll bet I can get more customers than you can. I'll stake my reputation on it.'

"The challenge startled Lysander. 'Your reputation? Ha! What everyone thinks of you isn't yours to bet,' exclaimed the rambunctious hare. 'No matter, I'll take you on anyway!' The neighbors scoffed, saying the sluggish tortoise didn't stand a chance. To prove it, they all agreed to judge the winner at this very spot in one week's time. As Lysander dashed off to make his preparations, Frank just sat still for a long time. Finally he ambled away.

"Lysander posted notices all over the countryside that he was cutting prices to less than half the price that Frank charged. Deliveries would be twice a day from now on, even on weekends and holidays. The hare passed through each neighborhood ringing a bell, handing out letters, selling stamps and supplies, and even weighing and wrapping parcels on the spot. For a small extra fee, he promised to deliver anytime, day or night. And he always gave a sincere, friendly smile at no extra charge. Being efficient, creative, and pleasant, the hare saw his customer list grow rapidly."

Davy was glued to the pictures and helped Grandma turn the pages as she continued reading aloud. "No one had seen any sign of the tortoise. By the end of the week, certain of victory, Lysander scurried up to meet the neighborhood judges. To his surprise he found the tortoise already there waiting for him. 'So sorry, Lysander,' said the tortoise in his glacial drawl. 'While you've been racing from house to house, I only have this one letter to deliver.' Frank handed Lysander a document and a pen adding, 'Please sign here on the dotted line.'

"'What's this?' asked Lysander.

"'Our king has appointed me, tortoise, Postmaster General and has authorized me to deliver all letters in the land. Sorry, hare, but you must cease and desist your deliveries.'

"'But that's not possible!' said Lysander, drumming his feet in a rage. 'It's not fair!'

"'That's what the king said, too,' answered the tortoise. 'It's not fair that some of his subjects should have better mail service than others. So he gave me an exclusive monopoly to insure the same quality of service for all.'

"Angrily, Lysander badgered the tortoise saying, 'How'd you get him to do this? What did you offer him?'

"A tortoise cannot smile easily, but he managed to curl up a scale at the side of his mouth. 'I have assured the king that he will be able to send all of his messages for free. And, of course, I reminded him that having all correspondence of the realm in loyal hands would make it easier for him to oversee the behavior of rebellious subjects. If I should lose a letter here or there, well, who's to complain?'

"'But you always lost money delivering the mail!' declared the hare irritably. 'Who'll pay for that?'

"'The king will set a price assuring my profits. If people stop mailing letters, taxes will cover my losses. After awhile no one will remember that I ever had a rival.'" Grandma looked up adding, "THE END."

"The moral of this story," read Rose, "is that you can always turn to authority when you have special problems."

Little Davy repeated, "'You can always turn to authority when you have special problems.' I'll remember to do that, Grandma."

"No, dear, that's only what it says in the book. It may be better for you to find your own moral."

"Grandma?"

"Yes, dear?"

"Can animals talk?"

"Only birds talk, child. This is just a fairy tale, not the Great Bard."

"Tell me about the Great Bard, Grandma."

She chuckled. "How many times have you heard it already? Bard is the wise condor who roams the seven seas, from the icy peaks of High Yek to the steamy shores of Roth. No, no, you won't trick me into another story. We'll save that for tomorrow."

Jonathan finished his meal and thanked the old couple for their gracious hospitality. As they all stepped out on the front stoop to say farewell, the old man told him, "Just think of us as your own grandpa and grandma if you ever need anything."

CHAPTER 19

BORED OF DIGESTION

efore he walked away, Jonathan asked for directions to the town hall. Rose looked worried and placed a hand on his arm, "Please, Jonathan, don't tell anyone about the meals that we served you. We don't have a permit."

"What?" said Jonathan. "You need a permit to serve meals?"

"In town, yes," she replied. "And it can be quite a problem for us if the authorities get word of our serving meals without a permit."

"What's the permit for?"

"It's to guarantee a certain standard of food for all. Years ago, townsfolk used to buy their food from street vendors, corner cafes, fancy restaurants, or they would get food at stores and cook in their own homes. Then the Council of Lords argued that it was unfair that some people should eat better than others and that people had to be protected from their own poor judgement. So they created political cafeterias where everyone in town could eat standard food for free."

"Not exactly free, of course," said Grandpa, pulling out his wallet and waving it slowly in front of Jonathan's nose. "The cost of each meal is much more than ever before, but nobody pays at the door. Uncle Samta paid with our taxes. Since meals at the political cafeterias, or 'politicafes,' were already paid for, a lot of people stopped going to private providers where they had to pay extra. With fewer customers, the private restaurants raised prices to cover expenses. Some survived with a handful of wealthy clients or with people on special religious diets, but most went out of business."

"Why would anyone pay for meals if they could go to politicafes for free?" wondered Jonathan aloud.

Rose laughed. "Because the politicafes became awful—the cooks, the food, the atmosphere—you name it! Bad cooks never get fired from politicafes. Their guild is too strong. And really good cooks are seldom rewarded because the bad cooks get jealous. The buildings are falling apart—filth and graffiti are everywhere. Morale is low, the food is bland, and the Board of Digestion decides the menu."

"That's the worst part," exclaimed Grandpa. "They try to please their friends and nobody's ever satisfied. You should have seen the fight over noodles and rice. Noodles and rice, day in and day out for decades. Then the spud lobby organized their campaign for bread and potatoes. Remember that?" he said, nodding to his wife. "When potato lovers finally got their people on the Board that was the last we ever heard of noodles and rice."

Davy made a choking sound. Peeking out from behind his grandmother's skirt, Davy's nose crinkled in disgust. "I hate potatoes, Grandma."

"Better eat 'em, dear, or the Nutrient Officers will get you."

"Nutrient Officers?" asked Jonathan.

"Shhh!" said Grandpa placing a finger to his lips. He looked over his shoulder and then down the street to see if anyone was watching. "Those who avoid politically approved meals usually fall into the hands of the Nutrient Officers. Kids call 'em 'nutes' for short. Nutes closely monitor attendance at meals and they hunt for anyone who fails to show up. Nutrient delinquents are taken to special detention cafeterias for forced feeding."

Davy shuddered. "But couldn't we just eat at home? Grandma's cooking is the best!"

"It's not allowed, dear," said Rose patting Davy on the head. "A few people have special permits, but Grandpa and I don't have the specified training. And we can't afford the elaborate kitchen facilities that would meet their requirements. You see, Davy, the Lords believe that they care more for your needs than Grandpa and I do."

"Besides," added Grandpa, "we both have to work in order to pay the taxes for all of this." Grandpa paced around the porch, half talking to himself, grumbling, "They tell us that we now have a lower digester-to-cook ratio than at any time in history, though half the population is functionally malnourished. The original plan to give better nutrition to the poor has ended with poor nutrition for all. Some misfits have refused to eat and seem on the verge of starvation, even though their food is free. Worse yet, vandals and gangsters roam the political cafeterias and no one feels safe there anymore."

"Please stop!" said Rose to her husband, seeing the shocked look on Jonathan's face. "He'll be scared to death when he goes to a politicafe." Turning to Jonathan she warned, "Just have your identity card ready when you show up at the door. You'll be all right."

"Thanks for your concern, Grandma Rose," said Jonathan, wondering what an identity card looked like and how he'd ever get food without one. "Would you mind if I pocketed a couple of extra slices of bread before leaving?"

"Why sure, dear. Have as many as you like." She went back into the kitchen and returned with several slices neatly wrapped in a napkin. She looked stealthily in both directions to see if any of her neighbors were watching, then proudly handed them to Jonathan saying, "Take good care of these. My son-in-law used to grow extra food for us, but the Food Police just..."

"I know," said Jonathan. "I'll be careful not to show this bread to anyone. Thanks for everything." With a good-bye wave, Jonathan stepped out on the street feeling warmed by the thought that, if necessary, he had a home in this forbidding island.

CHAPTER 20

"GIVE ME YOUR PAST OR YOUR FUTURE!"

 he town hall lay in the general direction of the square. Jonathan thought he could take a shortcut down an alley that was piled high with boxes and littered with trash. He hurried down the shaded alley, trying to ignore his feelings of unease after leaving the bright and busy street.

Suddenly Jonathan felt an arm at his throat and the cold metal of a pistol stuck between his ribs. "Give me your past or your future!" snarled the robber fiercely.

"What?" said Jonathan, shaking all over. "What do you mean?"

"You heard me—your money or your life," repeated the thief,

shoving the pistol deeper into his side. Jonathan needed no further encouragement. He reached into his pocket for his hard-earned money.

"This is all I have and I need half of the money to pay the tax collector," pleaded Jonathan, carefully hiding the slices of bread that Grandma Rose had given him. "Please leave me half."

The thief relaxed her grip on Jonathan. He could barely make out her face behind the scarf. In a low, harsh voice she laughed and said: "If you must part with your money, you're better off giving it all to me and none to the tax collector."

"Why?" he asked, placing the money in her dexterous, efficient hands.

"If you give the money to me," said the thief, stuffing the paper kayns into a leather pouch tied at her waist, "then at least I'll go away and leave you alone. But, until the day you die, the tax collector will take your money, the product of your past, and he'll use it to control everything about your future as well. Ha! He'll throw away more of your earnings in a year than all us free-lance robbers will take from you in a lifetime!"

Jonathan looked bewildered. "But doesn't the Council of Lords do good things for people with the tax money?"

"Oh, sure," she said dryly. "Some people become rich. But if paying taxes is so good, then why doesn't the tax collector just persuade you of the benefits and let you contribute voluntarily?"

Jonathan pondered this idea. "Maybe persuasion would take a great deal of time and effort?"

"Right," said the thief, showing her teeth with a grin. "That's my problem, too. We both conserve time and effort with a gun!" She spun Jonathan around with one hand and tied his wrists together with a thin cord, then pushed him to the ground and gagged him with his own handkerchief. "There. I'm afraid the tax collector will have to wait."

She sat down next to Jonathan, who wriggled but was unable to move. "You know what?" said the thief as she counted the money. "Politics is a kind of purification ritual. Most folks think it's wrong to covet, to lie, to steal, or to kill. It's just not neighborly—unless they can get a politician to do the dirty work for them. Yeah, politics allows everyone, even the best among us, to covet, to lie, to steal, and even to kill occasionally. And we can all still feel good about it."

Jonathan twisted his face and made some noises. The thief laughed, "So you'd like to yell, huh?"

Jonathan shook his head vigorously and, to her amusement, he looked up with mournful eyes. "Okay," she said, "Let's hear you whimper. But don't get too loud," she warned tapping the end of her pistol firmly against his nose. "I can make you very uncomfortable." She crouched at his side and jerked the handkerchief below his chin.

Stretching his jaw painfully, Jonathan challenged her, "But it's wrong to steal!"

"Maybe. The important thing is to do it in a really big way so that no one will notice that it's wrong."

"Steal a lot and no one will notice that it's wrong?"

"Sure. Little lies are bad. Children are taught not to be little liars. But really big liars can get streets named after them. If you steal a little bit you might go to the people zoo. But if you steal a whole lot, I mean the whole countryside, then you get your name engraved on buildings. Same with killing."

"Killing, too?" recoiled Jonathan.

"Where've you been?" snapped the thief. "Killing one or two people gets you time in the zoo or even executed. But killing a few thousand makes you a heroic conqueror worthy of songs, statues, and celebrations. Children are taught to admire and imitate big killers. Act small and you'll be scorned or forgotten. Act big and you'll be a legend in school books."

"The oldest story of robbery that I can remember," said Jonathan, "was of Robin Hood. He was a hero because he robbed from the rich and gave to the poor."

"Whom did he rob—in particular?" she asked.

"The Sheriff of Nottingham and his friends," recounted Jonathan. "You see the Sheriff and Prince John taxed everyone into poverty. The authorities took from both the rich and the poor. So Robin tried to return the plunder to the victims."

The thief laughed, "Then Robin wasn't a robber. How can you rob a thief?" She frowned and concentrated a moment. "That gives me an idea," she said. "I think I'll pay a visit to Tweed."

She abruptly replaced Jonathan's gag, adjusting it to be especially tight, and disappeared down the alley.

Jonathan lay helpless in the alley. He thought about the young policeman that he had met the day before. Where was that guy when he really needed him? How did the robber get a gun?

The thought of going back to the carnival in order to earn the money all over again angered Jonathan. He kicked his heels helplessly at the thought. One of the cords seared the skin on his wrist and Jonathan relaxed a moment to contemplate his predicament. He thought, "I never knew how good it felt to have my hands free—until now."

CHAPTER 21

THE BAZAAR OF GOVERNMENTS

onathan lay still in frustration. Mices reappeared, exploring garbage cans in the alley. He sniffed at the bread in Jonathan's pockets. But a noise at the end of the alley drove him back into hiding among the piles of junk.

A large brown cow sauntered toward Jonathan. "Moo-o-o," lowed the cow. The bell on her neck clanged slowly as she moved. Suddenly another cow appeared at the end of the alley, followed by a rugged old man with a staff. "Get back here, ya silly beast," grumbled the herdsman.

Jonathan wriggled and used his shoulder to nudge a box next to him.

The old man peered into the gloom. "Who's there?" Seeing Jonathan trussed and bound, he rushed over to pull off the gag.

Jonathan breathed relief. "I've been robbed. Untie me!" The old man reached into his pocket for a knife and cut the cords. "Thanks," said Jonathan, rubbing his sore wrists. He eagerly told the man what had happened.

"Yeah," said the rugged farmer, shaking his head. "You have to watch everyone these days. I would never have come to town except that I was told I could get help from the government."

"Do you think the government will help recover my money?" asked Jonathan.

"Not likely, but maybe you'll have better luck at the Bazaar of Governments than I did," replied the old herder. His face had more wrinkles than a prune and he wore rough clothes and rawhide boots. Jonathan felt reassured by his calm manner and direct speech.

"What's the Bazaar of Governments? Is it a place to sell cattle?" asked Jonathan.

The old man frowned and contemplated his two placid beasts. "That's what I came to find out," said the herdsman. "Actually, it's a kind of variety show. The building is fancier than a bank and bigger than anything I've ever seen. Inside are men peddling all sorts of governments to handle a citizen's affairs."

"Oh?" said Jonathan. "What kind of governments are they trying to sell?"

The herdsman scratched his sunburned neck and said, "There was this one feller calling himself a 'socialist.' He told me that his form of government would take one of my cows and give it to my neighbor. I didn't care much for him. I don't need any help giving my cow away to a neighbor—when it's necessary."

"Then there was this 'communist' in a bright red shirt. He had a booth next to the first peddler. Wore a big smile and kept shaking my hand, really friendly like, saying how much he liked me and cared for me. He seemed all right until he said that his government would take both of my cows. It'd be okay, he claimed, because everyone would own all the cows equally and I'd get some milk if he thought I needed it. And then he insisted that I sing his party song."

"Must be some song!" exclaimed Jonathan.

"Didn't have much use for him after that. I reckon he was going to skim most of the cream for himself. Then I wandered across the big hall and met a 'fascist' all dressed in black. Looked like he was on his way to a funeral." The old man paused long enough to shoo one of his cows away from a rancid mound of rubbish.

"That fascist also had a load of sweet talk up front and a lot of audacious ideas just like the other guys. Said he'd take both of my cows and sell me part of the milk. I says, 'What? Pay you for my own cow's milk?!' Then he threatened to shoot me if I didn't salute his flag right then and there."

"Wow!" said Jonathan. "I bet you got out of that place in a hurry."

"Before I could shake a leg, this here 'progressive' feller sidled up to me and offered a new deal. He told me that his government wanted to pay me to shoot one of my cows to reduce the supply. He'd milk the other, then pour some of the milk down the drain. Said he'd help me buy what was left at a nice high price. Now what crazy fool would go and do a thing like that?"

"Sure seems strange," said Jonathan, shaking his head. "Did you choose one of those governments?"

"Not on your life, sonny," declared the herdsman. "Who needs 'em? Instead of having them manage my affairs, I've decided to take my cows to the country market. I'll trade one of 'em for a bull."

CHAPTER 22

THE WORLD'S OLDEST PROFESSION

he old herdsman's tale left Jonathan more perplexed than ever. The Bazaar of Governments sounded intriguing, so he decided to go and see if anyone could help him get his money back.

"You can't miss it," said the old herdsman, preparing to lead his cows away. "It's in the Palace, the biggest thing on the square. You take the main portal—that's for you—flanked by two enormous windows. The window on the right is where people line up to pay their tax money in. The window on the left is where people line up to take tax money out."

"I can guess which line is more popular," joked Jonathan.

"That's for sure. Every month, one line gets a bit shorter and the other gets a bit longer." The old man tightened the hitches and gave a tug on the lead. "Eventually, when one line disappears, the other will too."

Sure enough, all streets led to the Town Square. On the square stood a magnificent palace. Words carved in stone over the huge entrance read: "PALACE OF LORDS." Mices, his tail standing straight up, had followed close to Jonathan's heels until he started up the broad steps leading into the building. The cat's back arched slightly and his hair bristled. This was as far as he would go.

Jonathan trotted up the steps until he stood before the grand entrance. Spread out before him was a gloomy hall with ceilings so high that the lamps could not light the interior completely. Just as the old herdsman described it, several booths lined the hall, displaying different banners and flags. People paced before the booths calling to every passerby and pressing pamphlets on them.

On the far side of the hall stood a great bronze door, flanked by large marble statues and fluted columns. Jonathan started to walk through the hall, hoping to avoid the sellers of governments. He had not moved two steps before a mature woman with gold bangles on her wrists and large earrings accosted him.

"Would you like to know your future, young sir?" she asked, approaching him.

Jonathan looked askance at this voluptuous woman wearing vividly colored scarves and heavy jewelry. He quickly checked his pockets, though he had nothing more to lose.

She continued aggressively, "I have the gift of foresight. Perhaps you'd like a glimpse of tomorrow to calm your fears of the future?"

"Can you really see into the future?" asked Jonathan backing off as far as he could without offending her. He regarded this brazen woman with deep suspicion.

"Well," she replied, her eyes flashed with confidence, "I study the signs and then I declare, affirm, and profess whatever I see to be true. Oh yes, mine is surely the world's oldest profession."

"Fortuneteller?" remarked Jonathan, suprised at the claim. "Do you use a crystal ball or tea leaves or..."

"Beelzebub, no!" snorted the woman with disgust. "I've become much more sophisticated. Nowadays I use charts and calculations." With a deep bow she added, "Economist at your service."

"How impressive. E-con-o-mist," he repeated slowly, rolling the long word over his tongue. "I'm sorry, I've just been robbed and I don't have any money to pay you."

She looked annoyed and turned away to look for other prospective clients.

"Please ma'am, could you tell me one thing," pleaded Jonathan, "even though I don't have anything to pay you?"

"Well?" said the woman, testily.

"When do people usually come to you for advice?"

She looked around to see if anyone might overhear them. Then, she whispered, "Because you have no money to pay me, I can let you in on a little secret. Clients come whenever they need to feel secure about the future. Whether the forecast is bright or gloomy—especially when gloomy—it makes people feel better when they can cling to someone else's prediction."

"And who pays for your predictions?" asked Jonathan.

"The Council of Lords is my best customer," she replied proudly. "The Lords pay me well—with other people's money, of course. Then they use my predictions in their speeches to justify the taking of more money to prepare for the murky future. It really works out well for both of us."

"That must be quite a responsibility," said Jonathan. "How accurate have your predictions been?"

"You'd be surprised at how few people ask me that," chuckled the economist. She hesitated and looked him carefully in the eye. "To be perfectly truthful, you might get a better prediction with the flip of a coin. The flip of a coin is something that anyone can do with ease, but it never does anyone any good. It will never make fearful people happy, it will never make me rich, nor will it ever make the Lords powerful. So you can see, it's important that I conjure impressive and complicated forecasts to suit them or they find someone else who will."

"Hmm," thought Jonathan. "It is the world's oldest profession."

CHAPTER 23

BOOTING PRODUCTION

 his must be the seat of power," said Jonathan to himself, staring in awe at the splendid marble statues and columns. "Why, they must have spent a fortune building this place!"

One great bronze door stood wide open and Jonathan could see a cavernous auditorium filled with people. Slipping in unobtrusively and standing in back, Jonathan could see a platform in the center. A group of disheveled and noisy men and women surrounded the platform waving their hands. In front of them stood a distinguished looking man who wore an expensive suit and drew occasional puffs on a fat cigar. He gestured with his cigar at one of the people in the crowd milling before him.

Jonathan crept closer to hear. One man, waving a pen in one hand and a pad of paper in the other, shouted over the others, "Your Honor, sir! Most esteemed High Lord Ponzi, sir! Is it true that you have just signed legislation to pay shoemakers not to produce shoes?"

"Ah-h-h, yes, it most certainly is true," answered Lord Ponzi, with an imperious nod. He spoke so slowly that he appeared to be waking from a deep sleep.

"Isn't this something of a path breaker, a precedent?" asked the man, scribbling furiously on his pad.

The High Lord solemnly nodded again in slow motion. "Uh, yes, this is a path break..."

A woman standing to the right of the first questioner interrupted before he could finish, "Is this the first time in the history of Corrumpo that shoemakers have been paid not to produce?"

"Yes," said Ponzi, "I do believe that is correct."

From the back, someone shouted, "Would you say that this program will help raise the prices of all kinds of footwear—shoes, boots, sandals, and so on?"

"Uh, yes, well—would you repeat your question?"

Another voice called out, "Will it raise shoe prices?"

"It will raise the income of shoemakers," replied the Lord, who nodded ponderously. "We certainly hope to do all we can to help the shoemakers in pursuit of a reasonable standard of living."

Jonathan thought of Davy and his mom. "How much harder it'll be to buy shoes from now on!"

Then a reporter, kneeling and mostly hidden by the throng, shouted from the very front of the platform, "Can you say what your program will be next year?"

Ponzi mumbled, "Uh, hmm, what did you say?"

"Your program. What's your plan for next year?" asked the reporter impatiently.

"Of course," said the High Lord, pausing to draw deeply from his cigar. "Uh huh. Ahem. Well, I believe that it is appropriate for me—to take the opportunity of this special press conference—to announce that next year we plan to pay everyone on the great island of Corrumpo not to produce anything."

There was a collective gasp from the audience. "Everyone?" "No kidding?" "Wow, that'll cost a fortune." "But will it work?"

"Work?" said Lord Ponzi, shaking himself out of his torpor.

"Will it stop people from producing?"

"Oh sure," he barely concealing a yawn. "We've had a pilot project in our front agency for years, and," said the Lord, a note of sleepy pride crept into his voice, "We've never produced anything."

At that moment, someone came up beside High Lord Ponzi and announced the end of the conference. The group of reporters surrounding the platform dissolved, abandoning the crowd seated in the auditorium. Jonathan blinked hard twice when he noted an almost imperceptible, sudden droop in Ponzi's posture—as if someone had snipped a string overhead that was holding him erect. The house lights dimmed as Ponzi was led off stage to a smoke-filled, back room.

CHAPTER 24

THE APPLAUSOMETER

lone spotlight cast a circle of light on the empty platform and the audience began to murmur. Someone began to clap rhythmically and soon the crowd joined in. The whole place reverberated with excitement and sound. At last, a robust figure with slick, jet-black hair, leaped onto the platform. He wore a glittering gold sequined suit and the silliest smile that Jonathan had ever seen. The man bounded back and forth like a cat across the stage as he greeted the excited crowd.

"Welcome, welcome, welcome! I'm Showman Phil and I'm thrilled to have you wonderful people here with me today on our show, 'You Are There!' And what a show we have for you, too. Later we'll be talking to—you guessed it—the Candidate!" Scantily clad women standing on both sides of the stage started waving their hands wildly and the whole crowd broke into thunderous applause.

"Thank you, thank you, thank you very much. First, I have a very, very, very special treat for you. We have none other than the Chairperson of the Corrumpo Election Commission here with us to explain the revolutionary new election procedures that we've all been hearing about." At this point, the host turned and, with a grand sweep of his arm up stage, yelled, "Will you all please welcome Doctor Julia Pavlov!"

The stagehands and the crowd again clapped wildly, cheering and whistling their excitement. Showman Phil shook Dr. Pavlov's hand and signaled for silence. "Well, well, Dr. Pavlov, you certainly seem to have built quite a following over the years."

"Thank you, Phil," she said. Dr. Pavlov wore thick spectacles, a stiff gray suit, and a look of calm assurance on her squarish face. "I'd say it's about 5.3 enthusiasm."

"Hey, hey, you've got me there," said the host. The stage assistants flashed a sign to the audience and they all let out a slight burst of laughter. "What do you mean '5.3 enthusiasm'?" asked Phil.

"Well," said Dr. Pavlov, "I have here an official applausometer. I always carry one around with me. It tells me just how much enthusiasm is shown by crowds of people."

"That's incredible, isn't it folks?" On cue, the crowd again eagerly applauded.

As soon as the noise subsided, Dr. Pavlov continued, "That's about 2.6."

"Amazing!" said the host. "What are you going to do with the applausometer? Are you using it in the next election?"

"That's right, Phil. We at the Corrumpo Election Commission have decided that counting votes is not enough. It's not just numbers that are important in deciding morality, power, wealth, and rights. We also feel that enthusiasm should count too."

"That's incredible!" shouted Showman Phil. Everyone broke into applause.

"4.3," said Dr. Pavlov passively.

"How are you going to do this, Doctor?"

Her thick eyebrows rose above her glasses and the first glimmer of a smile crossed her stern face. "This will be the first year to use applausometers at the election polls in the city. Instead of filling out ballots, voters will just stand in booths and applaud when a light comes on next to the name of the candidate of their choice."

"What do the candidates think of this new balloting procedure?" asked Phil.

"Oh, they love it, Phil. It seems that they have already been getting their supporters ready for the changeover. They spend long sessions promising to spend other people's money on their supporters and the promises always bring down the house."

"Well, thank you very much for being with us today and giving us a preview of a better tomorrow. Join us again, won't you? Ladies and gentlemen, let's hear it for Doctor Julia Pavlov!"

When the applause finally died down again, the host made another sweep of his hand toward the back of the stage. "Now for the moment you've all been waiting for. Yes, right off the busy, busy campaign trail— here's Joe Candidate! Let's hear it!"

Joe Candidate bounded athletically across the stage with both arms wide, beaming incandescently to the crowd. The candidate wore a stark black-and-white checkered suit. Jonathan thought he had the blackest hair and whitest teeth ever to shine under a spotlight. "Thank you, Phil. This is a really great moment for me to be here with all you fine people."

"Now Joe, you've just got to tell us the story behind the big story. You surprised everyone and hit the headlines with the hottest news in the island in over a decade. So what's the scoop?"

"Right to the point, huh, Phil? I like that about you and your show!

You see, I became alarmed at the tremendously high cost of political campaigns in recent years. So I decided to do something about it. I firmly believe that the voters of this great island deserve a bargain price for more of the same. That's when I started the Generic Party."

"The Generic Party! What a brilliant idea! And you even changed your own name, didn't you?"

"That's right, Phil. With my real name, Elihu Root, I could never really be the true people's candidate. You've got to cover your roots..." The impromptu pun drew a roar of laughter from everyone, including Phil and Joe. "But seriously, Phil," continued Joe, "you must have broad appeal if you're going to be credible."

"What are you doing to get the word out, Joe?"

"The Generic Party will soon have its basic black-and-white flyers, buttons, and posters available at all local outlets. We hope to cut the typical campaign budget in half with our ideas."

Showman Phil interrupted, "But do you have a stand on the issues?"

"Sure, just like all the other parties," said Joe. He reached inside his checkered coat and pulled out a sheaf of papers. "Here's our White Paper on Crime and here's our White Paper on Poverty."

"But, Joe, there's nothing on these white papers," said Phil, with an incredulous look. The White Papers were simply plain sheets of white paper.

"That's the beauty of it, Phil. Don't you see? Why waste time promising everything to everyone? Why not let voters fill in the papers themselves? Promises and performance will be just as before—only we save the cost of printing."

"How ingenious! While other candidates talk about cutting campaign costs, you really do something about it. Well, our time is running out. Can you sum up what your party is all about?"

"Sure, Phil. It's already catching on all across the island. Our slogan for the Generic Party is, 'We Believe What You Believe!'"

"Thank you very much, Joe. Ladies and gentlemen, can we have a really great round of applause, a high 5.5, for that genius of the campaign trail, Joe Candidate!"

CHAPTER 25

TRUE BELIEVER

As the applause began to fade, Joe Candidate just stood there motionless. Eager to keep the action rolling, Showman Phil tapped Joe on the arm and nudged him toward the exit. Joe just smiled and wouldn't budge. So Phil raised his arms to silence the audience.

Joe spoke up. "I have someone I want you to meet."

"Sure, Joe, of course, but we don't have much time."

"It'll only take a minute. I have to tell you about one of our generic voters—our number one generic voter." Joe turned to the side and motioned to someone offstage. No one appeared but Joe continued to gesture gently, as if coaxing a shy toddler. Finally, a pale, elderly woman appeared, at first gripping a fold of the curtain, then tentatively stepping forward.

Phil immediately dashed over to welcome this small figure and pull her forward. "Ladies and gentlemen," said Phil nervously, the shyness of the woman showing up his false ebullience, "aren't we lucky to have a bonus today? And who have we here?"

The old woman, wearing a simple black-and-white checkered dress, made Joe look like a caricature. Her pale face was nearly expressionless, her eyes blank and empty. Her salt-and-pepper gray hair was neatly combed over her ears. She gripped tightly a little black-and-white bag, as if it held her most valuable treasures.

When she reached Joe, he began to speak evenly. "As you know, Phil, the island's voting record has been dismal for years, but that hasn't discouraged our guest, Phoebe. Phoebe just happens to be the record-breaking voter in Corrumpo!"

Phil's eyes widened in astonishment. "Oh, I know about you! I've heard so much about you, ma'am. This is none other than the reigning voter of all time; the record holder of balloting; the champion of island mandates. Ladies and gentleman, we are truly blessed with the presence of none other than, Phoebe Simon!"

Again, the crowd responded to its handlers with generous applause, though some were sneaking out the back door. Others covered their yawns behind their programs.

"Phoebe," said Showman Phil, "I have a question that I'm sure is on everyone's mind." And he paused. Stillness descended on the auditorium. Projecting his voice so that everyone would hear, he said, "Why do you vote so consistently?"

With a look of pure innocence, Phoebe replied in a soft, sweet voice, "Well, sir, it's my duty to vote—this the Council tells me so. They say it doesn't matter who I vote for, so long as I vote. So, I vote. I have voted every single election since I was first eligible fifty years ago today."

"Wow!" replied Phil. "Fifty years! Isn't that incredible, folks!" Once again the audience clapped. "But let me ask you the ultimate voter question, Phoebe. There's a saying: 'The lesser of two evils is still evil.' Now tell me truthfully, Miss Simon, do you vote even when you don't like any of the candidates?"

"All the time, sir. My daddy once told me that if I didn't vote, then I'd have no right to complain about elected officials. I vote to protect my right to complain."

"How about that, folks! Now tell me honestly, Miss Simon, do you believe Joe's promises?"

"Of course, I believe. I always believe. If I didn't believe, why would I vote for him?"

"Do you know what the pundits are saying about you? They claim that you are the last true believer on Corrumpo?"

"Yes, sir, I've heard about them," Phoebe replied almost too softly to be heard. "I believe them, too. I believe you. I believe everyone."

Turning to the crowd, Phil placed a hand over his heart and exclaimed, "Ladies and gentlemen, have you ever heard anything so tender, so childlike. Isn't it wonderful that innocence can still be found on our all-too-cynical island." Then returning to his guest he asked, "And, Phoebe Simon, did your representative ever fail you?"

"Oh sure," shuddered Phoebe, "He always fails. Time and time again. He has hurt me so many times. But I stand by my rep, no matter what." She seized Joe's arm and pressed tightly to him. "And I will forever. I can't imagine life without Joe and all my ex-reps before him!"

Then someone from the audience shouted, "Why believe after so much heartache?"

She looked at Joe painfully and replied, "I believe that he is good at heart. He means well. I believe he can change—I can help him change. I believe that deep down he really cares about me. He just doesn't understand me."

"Aww!" sighed the audience in unison.

"Folks, this brings tears to my eyes. But, Phoebe, these are tears of concern as much as of joy. Some in your family have tried to get you to join Voters Anonymous."

"Oh no, sir!" she said shrinking. "Voters Anonymous is for people with a problem. I don't have a problem. Do you think I have a problem?"

"Phoebe, some experts declare that abused voters always keep returning to their reps no matter how much they suffer."

Looking up at Joe trustingly she asked, "Do I have a problem, Joe? I don't think so." Seeing him smile, she gushed, "I stand by my rep."

A bell rang off stage alerting Phil that they were out of time. Phil shouted for all to hear, "Where would we be without true believers like Phoebe Simon? Well, ladies and gentlemen, that's all the time we have. Thank you so much for joining us. Let's all show Phoebe Simon and Joe Candidate how much we love them both!"

The crowd broke into an enthusiastic cheer, happy that the real show was about to begin.

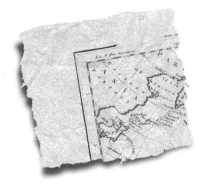

CHAPTER 26

ACCORDING TO NEED

 reat fanfare from trumpets and a resounding drum roll silenced the crowd. Showman Phil lifted his arms toward the audience, "You parents out there have been waiting long enough. Here's our finale. Your child's twelve-year trek is about to end. It's the Graduation Game!"

Organ music filled the great hall and side doors suddenly opened along the aisles. Through them marched students in mortarboards and long black gowns. The crowd broke into another raucous round of applause occasionally interspersed with whoops and hollers.

Jonathan whispered to a woman who was standing next to him, "What's the Graduation Game?"

She half-turned her head toward him and replied, "This is a contest among the youth of our Council schools." She paused briefly to listen to the announcements and then continued, straining to be heard over the noise. "It's the culmination of one's formal education. Until now, the purpose of a formal education has been to demonstrate the importance of hard work and diligent performance in the pursuit of knowledge. Tonight we honor the top students for their competitive success and outstanding achievements. But the ultimate prize, not yet awarded, is the Valedictory Trophy that goes to the winner of the Graduation Game."

Squinting at the stage, Jonathan saw a thick figure that looked familiar. "Who's that greeting the students as they step forward?"

"Why, that's Lady Bess Tweed. Don't you recognize her from the newspapers? She's our distinguished speaker. As a member of the Council of Lords and the queen of politicians, she's the guest of honor, as always, and she loves the publicity. Her profession is simultaneously the most revered and the least respected in the island. So, she's perfect for the Graduation Game."

"How's the game played?" asked Jonathan.

"It works like this," said the woman, pressing close to Jonathan's ear. "Lady Tweed gives one of her usual prepared political speeches. The students write down all the phrases that directly contradict what they have practiced or learned in school. The one who finds the most contradictions is declared the winner of the prestigious Valedictory Trophy. Shhhh, Lady Tweed has begun. Listen."

"...thus, we have learned about the virtues of freedom," bellowed Lady Tweed. "We know how free will and personal responsibility lead to maturity and growth. There you have it and that is the pressing situation for our fine community. People throughout history have always sought liberty. How wonderful it is that we now live on a free island..."

The woman pointed to the students behind Lady Tweed on the stage. "See how they are writing furiously. Oh, so many points to rack up!"

"Did Lady Tweed contradict what the students were taught in school?" asked Jonathan.

The woman snickered, "Free will? Nonsense. School is compulsory. Kids are forced to attend and everyone is forced to pay for it. Now hush!"

"...and we are fortunate to have the finest schools imaginable, especially as we face the harsh times that are forecast by our best economists," said Lady Tweed in ringing tones. "Our teachers are the model of exemplary behavior for our students, shining a path to democracy and prosperity with the light of truth and knowledge..."

The woman standing next to Jonathan grabbed his sleeve in excitement. She squealed, "My daughter is the third student from the right in the second row. She's writing; she's got all those points, I'm sure."

"I don't understand," asked Jonathan. "What points?"

"Finest schools? Impossible to compare without choice. Lady Tweed privately sent her own children to the countryside for lessons, but authorities assigned our kids to the nearest Council school. Model teachers? Ha! Students must sit quietly and take orders for twelve years. In return, they get letter grades and paper stars. If a teacher got paper stars instead of a paycheck, he'd call it slavery and go on strike! 'Shining a path to democracy?' No way! What they practice in class is autocracy."

Lady Tweed bowed her head humbly, "...now you have arrived at this milestone in your life. Each of us realizes that ours is but one small voice in the great human chorus. We know that fierce competition and a ruthless, greedy struggle to reach the top is unsuitable in today's world. For us, the noblest virtue is sacrifice. Sacrifice to the needs of others, to the multitudes who are less fortunate..."

The woman almost shrieked with delight. "Look at those students go! What a gold mine of contradictions! 'Great human chorus'? 'Sacrifice'? In school, they were always taught to excel, to be their own personal best. And Tweed, herself, is no slouch. She's the loudest, most demanding and unscrupulous of the lot. She has succeeded in clawing her way into the leadership by every cunning trick imaginable. These students know that they didn't get to this stage today by sacrificing their grades to the incompetent students around them."

Jonathan just could not figure this out. "You mean, in school the students are told to excel personally. And yet, upon graduation, Lady Tweed tells them to sacrifice themselves to others?"

"Now you've got it," replied the woman. "Lady Tweed preaches a changed world for graduates. From each according to ability and to each according to need. That's their future."

"Couldn't they try to be consistent and teach the same thing before and after graduation?" asked Jonathan.

"The authorities are working on that," said the woman. "The schools function on an old-fashioned tradition that awards high grades for the best performance. Next year they plan to reverse the grading system. They plan to use incentives and rewards that prepare students for the new reality. Grades will be awarded on the basis of need rather than achievement. The worst students will get A's and the best students will get F's. They say the worst students have more need of good grades than the best students."

Shaking his head, Jonathan repeated her words to make sure he heard them correctly, "The worst students will get A's and the best students will get F's?"

"That's right," she nodded.

"But what will happen to performance? Won't everyone try to become more needy and less able?"

"What matters, according to Tweed, is that this will be a bold, humanitarian act. The best students will learn the virtue of human sacrifice and the worst students will be instructed in the virtue of assertiveness. School officials have also been urged to adopt the same plan for teacher promotions."

"How did the teachers like that?" asked Jonathan.

"Some loved it and some hated it. My daughter tells me that the better teachers threatened to quit if the plan is adopted. Unlike the students, the teachers still have the luxury of that choice—for now."

CHAPTER 27

ШAGEſ OF ſIN

onathan left the cheering mob in the Palace auditorium and wandered down a long corridor. At the far end, rows of people sat on benches, all chained together with leg irons. Were these criminals awaiting trial? Perhaps the officials here might be able to recover his stolen money.

To the left of one bench was a door with the title, "Bureau of Hard Labor." At the far side of the bench uniformed guards stood talking quietly, ignoring their passive prisoners. The sturdy chains on these captives ensured that there was little hope of escape.

Jonathan approached the nearest prisoner, a boy of about ten who looked not at all like a criminal. "Why are you here?" asked Jonathan innocently.

The boy looked up at Jonathan and glanced furtively at the guards before answering, "I was caught working."

"What kind of work could get you into trouble like this?" asked Jonathan, his eyes wide with surprise.

"I stocked shelves at Jack's General Merchandise Store," replied the boy. He was about to say more, then he hesitated and looked up at the gray-haired man sitting next to him.

"I hired him," said Jack, a sturdy middle-aged man with a deep voice. The merchant still wore the stained apron of his trade—and leg irons attached to one of the boy's legs as well. "The kid said he wanted to grow up and be like his dad, a manager at the factory warehouse. Nothing more natural than that, you might say. When the factory closed, his dad had trouble finding a job. So I thought a job for the boy might do his family some good. I have to admit it was good for me, too. The big stores were driving me into the ground and I needed some cheap help. Well, it's all over now." A look of resignation crept over his face.

The young boy piped up, "At school they never paid me to read and to do arithmetic. Jack does. I handled inventory and the books—and Jack promised if I did well he'd let me place orders. So I started reading the trade journals and notices. And I got to meet folks, not just the kids at school. Jack promoted me and I helped my dad pay the rent—even earned enough to buy a bicycle. If I was paid nothing, I would've been praised for volunteering. But I got paid so now I'm busted," his voice trailed off as he stared at the ground, "and I've got to go back to make-believe."

"Make-believe ain't so bad, sonny, when you consider the alternative," declared a hefty, jovial man with a basket full of drooping white gardenias. He wore chains attached to the other leg of the boy. "It's tough to make a living. I've never liked working for anyone else. Finally, I thought I had it made with my flower cart. I did pretty well selling strings of pikaki and plumeria in the Town Square. People liked my flowers—the customers, that is. But the shopkeepers didn't much like the competition. They got the Council of Lords to outlaw 'peddlers.' A peddler! Yeah, that's what they call me because I can't afford a shop. Otherwise I'd be a 'shopkeeper' or a 'merchant.' I don't mean any offense, Jack, but my kind of selling existed long before your shop. Anyway, they called me a nuisance, an ugly eyesore, a bum, and now an outlaw! Can you figure me and my flowers being all that? At least I wasn't livin' off charity."

"But you sold right on the sidewalks," responded Jack. "You've got to leave 'em open for my customers."

"Your customers? You own the customers, Jack? Yeah, sure, I was on Council property. It's supposed to belong to everyone, but it doesn't, right Jack? It really belongs to those favored by the Lords."

Jack scoffed, "But you don't pay the steep property taxes that we have to pay as shopkeepers!"

"So who's to blame for that? Not me!" retorted the peddler irritably.

Jonathan intervened with a question, hoping to cool the debate. "So they arrested you on the spot?"

"Oh, I got a few warnings first. But I didn't care to dance to their tune. Who do they think they are, my masters? I'm trying to work for myself, not some nosey boss. Anyway, the zoo's okay. I don't have to work and I get three squares a day and a room at the shopkeepers' expense. Oddly enough, the warden thinks he's doing me a favor. Says he's going to rehabilitate me so I can make a contribution to society. He's talking taxes, not flowers."

The young boy began to whimper. "Do you think they'll send me to the zoo, too?"

"Don't worry, kid," soothed the flower seller. "If they do, you're sure to learn a practical trade."

Jonathan turned to a group of women wearing overalls who sat next in line. "Why are you here?"

"We have a small fishing boat. Some official stopped me as I lifted some heavy crates down at the dock," said a wiry, rugged woman with piercing blue eyes. "He told me I violated the safety regulations." Motioning to her companions, she added, "The regulations supposedly protect us from abuse in the work place. The officials shut us down twice, but we sneaked back to the docks to get the rigging ready for the coming season. They caught us, again, and said that this time they're going to protect us real good behind bars."

She wondered aloud, "What will they do with my son? He's only three and he weighs more than those crates that I lifted. Nobody complained when I carried him around!" Fighting back her tears she added, "Now they'll have to find someone else to carry him."

"Finding someone else is not so easy," said a man whose full beard barely concealed a pockmarked face. Elbowing the youth next to him on the bench, he said, "George has been working part-time for me two winters in a row, sort of an apprentice. He helps keep my barbershop clean and readies all the customers. When I tried to teach him the trade, we got into trouble because he's not yet a member of the guild." He threw up his hands in exasperation.

Young George, with a mournful look on his face, lamented, "At this rate, and now with a court record, I'll never get my license."

CHAPTER 28

NEW NEWCOMERS

ou think you have problems?" said a haughty looking woman, clearly distressed that she was chained to people she considered her inferiors. On the verge of tears, she pressed a fine lace handkerchief to her eyes and said, "When the press finds out that I, Madam Ins, am under arrest, my husband's career will be finished. I never thought I was doing anything so wrong. What would you have done?"

Embracing a young couple chained next to her, Madam Ins continued, "Years ago, I had a big home, three kids who attended the finest schools, and I wanted to get back to my career. My neighbor traveled a lot so I asked him to keep an eye out for people who might help with my household. He highly recommended Jiyo and Shar, so I hired them immediately. Shar is wonderful with the garden and carriage. She can fix anything around the house and does endless errands."

"And Jiyo, such a dear, has been my lifesaver. He's so good with the kids. He's always there when I need him. He cooks, cleans, cuts hair— does a thousand and one chores better than I ever could. My boys are crazy about his cookies. When I get home I can relax with my husband and play with the kids."

"Sounds like help that everyone would love to have," said Jonathan. "What went wrong?"

"Everything was just fine at first. Then my husband got a new appointment to head the Bureau of Good Will. His opponents investigated our finances and found that we had never paid the retirement taxes for Jiyo and Shar."

"Why not?" asked Jonathan.

"With taxes high and my earnings low, we couldn't afford to at the time. And they're not allowed to collect the retirement benefits anyway."

Jiyo spoke up saying, "Report is very trouble for us."

His wife poked him and whispered, "Careful, Jiyo. Much risk."

To his wife, Jiyo replied bravely, "Madam help us. We help her now." Then to Madam Ins he said, "You save our lifes. We come from home island of El Saddamadore. Very bad hunger and very bad war. We no choice—leave, hunger, or be kill. So we come Corrumpo. Madam no help us, we die."

"This true," said Shar, in a mild voice. "Now sorry we give Madam trouble."

Madam Ins heaved a great sigh and said, "My husband will lose his promotion to the Bureau of Good Will and maybe his old job, as well. He has been the head of the Us First Commission, promoting national pride. His enemies will accuse him of hypocrisy."

"Hypocrisy?" asked Jonathan.

"Yes. The Us First Commission discourages new newcomers."

"*New* newcomers?" repeated Jonathan. "Who are the *old* newcomers?"

"Old newcomers? That's the rest of us," said Madame Ins. "This is an island. Over the years, all of our ancestors came from somewhere else as newcomers, either fleeing oppression or trying to improve life. But new newcomers are recent arrivals. They're banned by the Pulluptheladder Law."

Jonathan swallowed uneasily. He dared not think of what would happen if the authorities discovered that he was a new newcomer as well. Trying to sound only mildly interested, he asked, "Why don't they want new newcomers?"

The fisherwoman interrupted, "New newcomers are allowed if they spend money and leave right away. They're tourists or businessmen. But the Council of Lords worries about poor new newcomers, ones who might stay. Many work harder, longer, cheaper, smarter, or at greater risk than the locals. They'll do chores that Madame Ins wouldn't touch."

"Hold on just a minute!" said Jack. "There are plenty of legitimate complaints against new newcomers. New newcomers don't always know the language, the culture, or the manners and customs of our island. I admire their spirit—they're gutsy to risk their lives to come here as strangers—but it takes time to learn everything and there's not enough space. It's more complicated than when our ancestors fled the far islands."

Jonathan thought about all the space he had seen on Corrumpo, all the uninhabited forests and open fields. Most people avoided the wilderness and preferred the crowds and activity of city life.

Then Madam Ins answered Jack, "My husband made those very same arguments against new newcomers. He always said that new newcomers must first learn our language and customs before they can be allowed to stay. They must also have money, skills, self-sufficiency, and they shouldn't take up any space. My husband drafted a new law to identify and deport people that didn't qualify, but there was a glitch. The description of illegal new newcomers applied more to our own kids than to talented people like Jiyo and Shar."

Two men in stiff uniforms barged through the doors, each man being tugged by a ferocious black dog on a leash. They marched directly up to Madam Ins, who shrank in fright from the dog's heavy panting and drooling fangs. One of the men motioned for the guard to unlock her leg irons. In a deep monotone, he read from a document, "Dear Madame Ins,

We wish to axtend..." He paused to show the letter to the other man, whispered, then started again. "Dear Madame Ins, We wish to *extend* our sincere apologies for this unfortunate misunderstanding. Madame Ins, you can be assured that this whole matter is being taken care of at the highest levels."

Visibly relieved, she hastily followed her escorts down the long hall without daring to look back at Jiyo or Shar. The rest watched in a dead silence that was broken only by the clank of a restless chain. Once Madam Ins was out of sight, the guards turned on Jiyo and Shar, unlocking and separating them from the group and from each other. Roughly shoving them in the opposite direction, the guards yelled, "Off you go, scum. Back to where you came from."

"We no harm!" pleaded Shar. "We die!"

"That's none of my doing," grumbled the guard.

The fisherwoman waited until they turned down the stairwell and the door slammed behind them, then she mumbled under her breath, "Yes it is."

Jonathan trembled slightly, thinking of the fate that lay ahead for the couple and maybe even for himself. He looked up and asked the woman, "So everyone on this chain is here because they weren't allowed to work?"

Pointing down the row to one young man whose face was buried in his hands, the woman responded, "If you look at it that way, he's the exception. The authorities insisted that he sign up to work as a soldier. He refused—so he got locked on this chain with the rest of us."

Jonathan couldn't quite see the face of the young man, yet he wondered why the town elders would require one so young to do their fighting for them. "Why do they force him to be a soldier?"

The fisherwoman answered Jonathan, "They say it's the only way to protect our free society." Her words echoed in Jonathan's ears, amidst the metallic noise of the chains.

"Protect from whom?" asked Jonathan.

Glowered the woman, "From those who would put us in chains."

CHAPTER 29

TREAT OR TRICK?

he Palace of Lords had more rooms and halls than a labyrinth. Jonathan began to smell something delicious—coffee and fresh baked bread! He followed his nose down a corridor and into a great meeting hall where several elderly men and women stood arguing and angrily shaking their fists. Some held the hands of others who wept quietly.

"What's the matter?" asked Jonathan, who noticed a huge basket sitting in the center of the hall. It reached almost to the ceiling. "Why are you so upset?"

Most of the old folks ignored him and continued moaning and complaining to each other. But one serious fellow stood up slowly and approached Jonathan. "That uppity Lord," he grumbled, "he's done it again! He fooled us!"

"What did he do?" asked Jonathan.

"Years ago," the old man remarked sarcastically, "High Lord Ponzi told us of a grand scheme to prevent anyone from ever going hungry in their old age. Sounds good, huh?"

Jonathan nodded in agreement.

"Yeah, that's what we all thought, too. Humph!" he snorted with exasperation. "Upon pain of death, everyone, except that high and mighty Carlo Ponzi and his Council, received the order to contribute loaves of bread into this gigantic basket every week. They call it the Security Trust Basket. Those who reached sixty-five years of age and retired could start taking bread out of the Security Trust Basket."

"Everyone except Lord Ponzi and his Council contributed?" repeated Jonathan.

"Yeah, they got special treatment," responded the old man. "We had to put more of our own bread in a separate basket exclusively reserved for them. Now I know why they wanted their own kept separate."

"It must be nice to have bread for your old age," said Jonathan.

"That's what we thought, too. It seemed such a marvelous idea because there would always be bread to feed the elderly. Since we could all count on the great Security Trust basket, most of us stopped saving any bread of our own for the future. Figured we didn't have to help our family and neighbors either, since the Council would take care of us all."

His shoulders slumped as if weighed down by the burden of a lifetime. The old man scanned the frail and aged group. He pointed to another elderly gentleman who was seated on a bench nearby. "One day my friend, Alan, watched people put bread in and take bread out of the big basket. Alan calculated that the Security Trust Basket would soon be empty. He used to be a bookkeeper, you know. Well, Alan raised the alarm." Alan began to nod shakily.

"We went straight to that basket and climbed up the side. It took some doing, but we're not as weak and blind as some of those young Lords think. Anyway, we looked in and discovered that the food basket was almost empty. The news caused an uproar. We told that High Lord Ponzi right then and there that he'd better do something quick or we'd have his hide at the next election!"

"Whew, I bet he was scared," said Jonathan.

"Scared? I never saw anybody so fidgety. He knows we have a lot of clout when we get riled up. First he proposed to give the elderly even more bread, beginning just before the next election. Then he'd take more bread from the young workers, beginning right after the election. But the workers saw through his scheme and they got mad, too. Those young workers said they wanted to have bread now. They said their own pantries protected bread against mold and rats better than the Council's big basket. And they don't trust the Lords to leave the bread alone until they retire."

"What did he do then?" asked Jonathan.

"That Ponzi always has a new angle. He then said that everyone should wait five years longer, until seventy years old, before they could start taking bread out of the basket. Well, this angered those close to retirement, those who expected to collect bread at sixty-five as promised. Finally, Ponzi came up with a brilliant new idea."

"Just in time!" exclaimed Jonathan.

"Just in time for Election Day. Ponzi promised everybody everything! He'd give more to the elderly and take less from the young. Perfect! Promise more for less and everyone's happy!" The old man paused to see if Jonathan could see what was happening. "The catch is that the loaves will be smaller every year. Yup. The loaves of bread will be so small that we'll be able to eat a meal of a hundred loaves—and still feel hungry."

"Darn crooks!" burst Alan. "When those loaves are gone they'll have us eating pictures of bread!"

CHAPTER 30

WHOSE BRILLIANT IDEA?

ooray, hooray!" shouted a man at the top of his lungs. Startled, the elderly men and women stared in amazement at this loud disruption. The intruder was perfectly groomed, sporting a finely trimmed mustache and wearing the latest gentleman's fashion. He charged into the room, heading an entourage of men dressed in sleek dark suits, all carrying briefcases. They fawned over him as if their lives depended on him. Their leader strode over to the table for a cup of coffee, impatiently brushing off his followers with an imperious wave of his hand. Sheep-like, they withdrew to a corner of the room to await his summons.

"Congratulations," said Jonathan, "for whatever you're celebrating." Jonathan felt compelled to pour coffee for this dandy, while studying the sharp lines and precision of his clothing. "Do you mind my asking why you're so happy?"

"Not at all," the gentleman said proudly. "Thanks for the coffee. Ow! It's hot! Take a note of that, Number Two," he said to a follower who rushed up and pulled a notepad from his pocket. Setting the coffee back down, the gentleman stuck his hand out to Jonathan saying, "My name's George Selden. What's yours?"

"Jonathan. Jonathan Gullible. Pleased to meet you."

George shook Jonathan's hand firmly. "Jonathan, today my riches are assured. I just won a decisive vote."

"What vote?"

"By a vote of three to two, the High Court confirmed my letter patent for sharpmetalonastick."

"What's a letter patent?" asked Jonathan.

Thrusting his chest out proudly, George declared, "It's only the most valuable piece of paper on Corrumpo. The Council issued a letter giving me exclusive use of a revolutionary new idea for cutting timber. No one may use sharpmetalonastick without my permission. I'll be filthy rich!"

"When did you invent this?"

"Oh, I didn't come up with the idea. Charlie Goodyear, rest his soul, put the whole thing together and filed papers with the Bureau of Idea Control. He died before it came through and I paid Charlie's widow a pittance for the rights to his claim. It'll soon pay off!" Nodding over his shoulder at the flock of men huddled in the corner, George added, "Charlie couldn't afford to hire that crew of lawyers on his own."

"So, who lost the vote?" asked Jonathan.

"Lots!" George squinted at the ceiling, counting in his head. "Must be, well, at least thirty-four others claimed that they had thought of this thing before me, uh, before Charlie, that is. Some argued that it was the next logical discovery after stoneonastick. Ha! Charlie's grandmother even filed a counterclaim, saying she made his discoveries possible. And some science fiction writer tried to horn in saying that Charlie stole ideas from him."

George stopped long enough to blow on his coffee. "But this last court challenge was the toughest. The plaintiff claimed her father put metal to wood first. Can't even remember her name now."

Jonathan gulped, recalling his encounter with the tree workers. "Was the woman named Drawbaugh?" He remembered the first incident on the island with the woman tree worker.

"Doesn't matter, really. What's-her-name had more than twenty phony witnesses testify that she had the idea long ago. Said her father was a born tinkerer. Said she and her father were simply trying to make her work a little easier. Then she played on the sympathies of the judges by arguing that, as a poor tree worker, she didn't have money for patent fees and lawyers. But I spoiled it for her by revealing her recent arrest record. Shattered her credibility with the judges. Tough luck, huh?"

"Luck?" responded Jonathan.

"I suppose she wanted a place in the history books. Now, no one will ever hear of her." Putting his cup down again, George leaned against the wall and studied the perfectly manicured nails of his right hand, clearly relishing his moment of triumph. "Each of these challenges has a different twist," continued George. "Some say I can't own the use of an idea—that it deprives others of liberty. But the court says I can because Charlie was the first to file and there's no place for latecomers. I own it for seventeen years."

"Seventeen years? Why seventeen years?" asked Jonathan.

"Who knows?" he chuckled. "Magic number, I guess."

"But if you own the use of an idea, then why does it end after seventeen years? Do you lose all your property after seventeen years?"

"Hmmm." George paused and took up his coffee again. He began to stir it pensively. "Good question. There's usually no time limit on property ownership, unless the Council takes it for a higher social purpose. Maybe there's a higher social purpose. Wait a moment." He raised his hand and Number Two promptly came running from his corner of the room. This puppy of a man practically bounced to George's side.

"What can I do for you, sir?"

"Number Two, tell this young friend of mine why I can't own a letter patent for more than seventeen years."

"Yes, sir. Well, it's like this. In ancient times the letter patent simply gave royal monopolies to friends of the monarch. Today, however, the function of a letter patent," said Number Two in a droning monotone, "is to motivate inventors who, otherwise, wouldn't have any reason to invent useful things or to reveal their secrets. A century ago, a superstitious inventor persuaded the Council of Lords that six months less than two and a half seven-year apprenticeships allowed sufficient monopoly privileges to motivate inventors."

"Please correct me if I'm mistaken," said Jonathan, straining to understand. "You say that inventors are motivated solely by a desire to get rich by stopping others from using ideas?"

George and Number Two looked blankly at each other. George replied, "What other motive could there be?"

Jonathan found their lack of imagination a little depressing. "So every maker of sharpmetalonastick must pay you?"

"Either that or I produce them, myself—a few at a time and at great expense," said George.

Number Two laughed nervously, glancing sideways at George. "Ahem, well that's still uncertain, sir. We have staff looking into this already. You recall that we first have to deal with the bothersome Tree Workers Law prohibiting the use of new tools. Another meeting with Lady Tweed is scheduled later today. If we are successful at obtaining an exemption from the law, then perhaps the tree workers will make us an offer to sit on the idea for seventeen years."

Returning to Jonathan, Number Two explained, "The tree workers have a quaint, but archaic, notion that their use of an old idea should be protected from our use of a new idea. As they see it, we're the latecomers."

George was lost in thought. Speaking absent-mindedly he commented, "That Tree Workers Law is downright anti-progressive, don't you think Number Two? I know I can count on you. You're always ahead of the game."

"But, sir," persisted Jonathan, "what if you hadn't won your patent in court today?"

In a grand embrace, George hugged both Number Two and Jonathan around the shoulders, marching them toward the door. "Young man, without a patent, you can bet that I wouldn't be wasting time jabbering with you. I'd race for the best factory to turn out the best sharpmetalonastick faster than anyone else. And Number Two would be looking for another job. Right, Number Two? Maybe production, marketing, or research, instead of law. Every new sharpmetalonastick would have to carry the slightest innovation just to keep one step ahead of the pack!"

"Ugh! Sounds dreadful!" snickered Number Two. "No, I'd find opportunity in another area of law—contracts or fraud, perhaps."

CHAPTER 31

THE SUIT

eeing their leader, George, head for the door, the other men in the corner picked up their briefcases and followed close behind. "Number Two," said George, "explain that problem of liability to me again, would you?" George wanted to show Jonathan how well his lawyers performed.

The whole bunch marched rapidly down the hall with George's arms still slung around the necks of both Number Two and Jonathan. "You see," said Number Two, "the metal piece may fly off the stick and hit some bystander. So we have to protect you and the other investors."

"Protect me if the metal piece hits someone else? Whatever do you mean?" said George, feeding questions to the lawyer.

"The injured person might sue you in court, trying to get you to pay for damages—lost income, trauma, legal fees, etcetera, etcetera." The group practically stepped on Jonathan's heels as they tried to stick close to George. For the knee-walkers in the group, the pace was especially difficult, but they muffled their groans and consoled themselves with the thought of year-end tax returns.

"A lawsuit could ruin me!" said George, feigning alarm and watching Jonathan's reaction out of the corner of his eye.

Number Two continued, unaware that he was performing on cue. "So an ingenious new idea has been enacted by the Council of Lords to absolve you of personal responsibility for losses suffered by others."

"Another new idea? Who owns the letter patent on that?" said Jonathan innocently.

Number Two raised an eyebrow, then proceeded, ignoring Jonathan's question. "We file these forms and put the letters 'Lpr.' after your company name." Without missing a step, Number Two struggled to unbutton a folder to withdraw a stack of papers. "That reminds me, Mr. Selden, please sign on the line at the bottom."

Jonathan was fascinated. "What is 'Lpr.'?" he asked, stumbling a little to keep up.

"'Lpr.' means 'Limited personal responsibility,'" said Number Two. "If Mr. Selden registers his company, the most he can lose to a lawsuit is the money he invested. The rest of his wealth is safe from victims. It's a kind of insurance the Council sells for an additional tax. Since the Council limits the risk of financial loss, more people will invest in our company. And they'll pay less attention to what we do."

"At the worst," commented George, "we can shut down the company and walk away. Then we start another one under a new name. Pretty clever, eh?"

In that instant, George's eye caught sight of a stunning young woman coming down the hall. She had more curves than should be legally allowed on a public street and walked to emphasize each one. As he turned to watch her pass, George tripped, tumbling pell-mell, jamming his perfectly groomed fingers into the wall. "Ow!" he cried in agony, his arms and legs sprawling in every direction. He tried to raise himself up from the floor and complained of a sharp pain in his hand and lower back. His lawyers swarmed over him in a frenzy, exchanging words frantically. A few helped gather items that had fallen out of George's pockets while others busily jotted notes and drew diagrams of the scene.

"I'll sue!" yelled George, holding his bruised and bloody fingers in a silken handkerchief. "I'll crush the stinking lout who's responsible for this obstruction in the floor! And you, young lady, I'll see you in court for causing my distraction!" Quick as a flash, several lawyers darted over to the woman, calling for her name and address.

Shocked, the young lady purred haughtily, "Sue me? Do you know who I am?"

"I don't care," said George, glaring. "The bigger the better. I'll sue!"

Trembling and fighting to control her anger, she countered, "You can't do that! My boyfriend, Carlo, that's *Carlo Ponzi,*" she repeated for emphasis, "says my beauty benefits everyone—that it's a public good. He declared it so—he told me last night!" Instinctively, she reached into her purse to find a mirror. What she saw displeased her. Her eye makeup looked smeared. "Now look what you've done to a public good! Carlo says that everybody should pay for public goods. He always puts my cosmetics on his expense account. Well, you'll be sorry! Your taxes will go up because of this!" She stuffed the mirror back into her purse and stormed away in search of a powder room.

Feeling some sympathy for the woman, Jonathan asked, "Are you really going to sue her? How can she be blamed?"

Ignoring Jonathan, George crawled along the floor looking intently for a protrusion, evidence of negligence on someone else's part. He stopped at an indentation and screamed, "That's the cause, Number Two! Find out who's responsible. I'll have his job and every penny he owns. And what's that female's name?"

"Calm down, George," said Number Two. "That's Ponzi's girl. Forget her if you want to repeal the Tree Workers Law. However, this building is Palace property. With the Lords' permission, we can sue the taxpayers."

George smiled broadly and exclaimed, "Number Two, you're a

genius. Put it on the agenda for Tweed! Of course, the Lords don't care if we sue the Palace. The settlement money won't come out of their pockets. We'll even see that they get a share." He wondered how much Lady Tweed would extract from him for this favor. George's pain was fading rapidly. "This gives me a chance at the deepest pockets of all."

"You'll ask the Lords to pay for your injury?" asked Jonathan.

"No, you idiot," retorted George. "The Lords have the ultimate Lpr. No, they'll hand the innocent taxpayers to me on a silver platter. I'm going to collect big time!"

CHAPTER 32

DOCTRINAIRE

onathan followed George's entourage out the Palace of Lords in search of medical help. Across from the Palace, a long white building occupied most of the block. The group entered the nearest door. Suddenly screams of agony came from an open window halfway down the block. Dashing along the sidewalk, Jonathan reached the window just as the shutters were closing. He grabbed one of the shutters, holding it open.

"Get away," shouted a large matronly woman from inside. Her angry red face contrasted sharply with the white uniform that covered her from head to toe.

"What's going on in there?" insisted Jonathan. "What's the screaming about?"

"That's none of your affair. Now let go!"

In desperation, Jonathan tightened his grip. "Not until you let me know what you're doing! You're hurting someone!"

"Of course we're hurting someone," said the woman. "How else can we cure them? Trust me, I'm a doctor."

Sure enough, Jonathan saw the woman's name and title embroidered on her uniform—Dr. Abigail Flexner. Jonathan gasped, "You hurt people to cure them? Why don't you just let them alone?"

"We must kill the demons. Sometimes, we can't help it if the patient is hurt as well," declared the doctor matter-of-factly. Frustrated with Jonathan's stubbornness, she looked around for help in dealing with this impertinent youngster. "Oh, all right," she said resignedly. "I'll prove that we're helping people. Go around by the side door and I'll give you a little instructional tour."

Suspicious, Jonathan finally let go of the shutter and went where he was told. George and the others had passed through the same door, but Jonathan saw no sign of them inside. He had entered a room filled with people of all ages, sitting or standing shoulder-to-shoulder along the walls. Some moaned loudly and held out arms and legs wrapped with bandages and tied with splints. Others muttered, paced anxiously, or comforted loved ones. Many people had bedding and cooking utensils piled next to them, signs of a long occupation. Jonathan wondered how long these people had to wait.

Dr. Flexner opened an interior door and beckoned to Jonathan. The crowd immediately stopped all activity and grew hushed; the occupants stared enviously at Jonathan as he passed by in front of them. The doctor admitted him to a windowless room filled with desks, clerks, and piles of paper stacked to the ceiling. She guided him to another door, which led to a small amphitheater stage, ringed by a balcony with seats. The powerful odor of chemicals and decay assaulted Jonathan's senses.

Scores of observers leaned on the railing of the balcony. Below, several men and women in white, apparently doctors and nurses, huddled intently over a bulky patient strapped to a low table.

"To heal this patient," whispered the doctor somberly, "orthodox practitioners cut open veins to let the demons flow out with the blood. On occasion, we apply blood leeches." She pointed to a table next to the patient, which held an array of knives, saws, candles, and bottles of various sizes and shapes. Oozing over the side of a large metal bowl, slimy leeches, the size of a man's thumb, writhed. Jonathan felt his stomach turn.

"Failing that, our men and women of science poison the demons with chemicals. We prefer to use arsenic, antimony, and compounds of mercury. What great progress we have made in medical science! Mark my words, a century from now physicians will marvel at our achievements."

"Aren't those poisons deadly?" said Jonathan. He recalled that his uncle sold mixtures like these compounds to kill rats back home. He vaguely remembered hearing old-timers tell of such dangerous substances used medically in the old days. But hadn't those practices ended long ago?

"Can't be helped," she said reassuringly. "Cut, draw, and poison are the only safe and effective treatments."

"How often does it work?"

"The treatment succeeds in destroying demons one hundred percent of the time! And," she beamed, "our patients experience a stunning twenty-seven percent survival rate."

Jonathan stared. One of the doctors slit the patient's belly and gouts of blood spurted. "What's his ailment?"

"Opsonin rot of the nuciform sac," answered Dr. Flexner. "We're certain."

"Isn't there any other way to treat him?"

"Ha!" she snorted. "Some claim otherwise. Thank God those quacks aren't licensed to administer cures. It isn't enough just to certify the quality of our own physicians for people to choose. We must outlaw charlatans who pretend to heal with unauthorized medicines, silly diets, molds, plants, pins, touch, prayers, fresh air, exercise, and sometimes even, can you believe it," she scowled, "laughter! When we catch 'em we toss 'em in the zoo and throw away the key!"

"Do those cures ever work?" asked Jonathan softly.

"Pff! Mere coincidence if they do," she replied. Jonathan noticed her puffy and bloated face. Her blotched red nose provided the only color in her complexion, gray the color of an overcast sky. Her breath could kill.

"But what if a patient chooses those remedies?" prodded Jonathan. "Whose life is it?"

"Precisely!" she exclaimed. Jonathan had raised a favorite topic. The doctor drew Jonathan away from the railing and crossed her thick arms in front of her, one hand to her chin. Speaking fervently she said, "Whose life is it? Some of these selfish patients actually think that life is their own! They forget that each life belongs to all. All of us form an unbroken line from ancestors to descendants, all connected to the great whole. For the good of society, trained professionals must protect patients from their own poor judgement. Imagine! Some patients actually want to kill themselves! We're much better prepared to decide when and how they are to be treated."

She paused to reflect, then continued, "Besides, the Council of Lords generously pays all medical bills on the island. Healthy workers stand duty in the tax line, prioritized by the Council's judgement of ability. Patients stand duty in the wait line, prioritized by our judgement of need. The two lines must one day match, so we cannot afford to let patients make costly errors with the people's money."

A moan of pain resounded through the room and more blood squirted into a basin on the floor. Attendants relayed commands. The attending surgeon received more instruments and sponges. A concerned look clouded the doctor's face as she stood next to Jonathan. "I feel his pain," she murmured.

"How do you get a license," asked Jonathan, "so that you can make these life and death decisions for people?"

"It takes many, many years of preparation. One must undertake orthodox medical schooling, pass numerous tests. As authorized by our friends in the Council of Lords, we closed one of the two medical schools of Corrumpo in order to maintain high orthodox standards. Years of scholarly research and hallowed traditions provide these standards. The Benevolent Protective Guild of Orthodox Medicine awards licenses and assures practitioners of remuneration proper to their standing in society."

"High pay?" said Jonathan.

"That's all for now." The doctor gave an impatient look and ushered Jonathan out. But Jonathan refused to stop asking questions. "How do you know which doctor is good and which is bad?"

"We minimize opportunities for unhelpful choice and unnecessary speculation. There's no such thing as a bad doctor," she asserted. "Licensed doctors are all equally qualified. Of course there are rumors— we can't stop gossip about good and bad. But our control over the reports assures that any such gossip is baseless." Quick as a flash she pushed him out the back door and slammed it with a bolt.

CHAPTER 33

VICE VERSA

N o sooner had he exited the building than he nearly tripped over Mices, lying in wait outside with a dead rat at his feet. Eyeing the revolting rat, Jonathan mused, "I can imagine where this came from, Mices. Thanks, but no thanks." The yellow cat scratched his torn ear, unconcerned by Jonathan's rejection of the juicy rat.

Across the street, Jonathan noticed a woman wearing heavy makeup and a tight fitting, bright red dress. As a gentleman passed her on the street, she smiled and tried to engage him in conversation. She didn't appear to be begging. No, Jonathan thought she was trying to sell something. When unsuccessful in her efforts with the man, she abruptly turned to find another customer. Jonathan wondered if Lord Ponzi had declared this gaudy woman a public good, too.

Then, coming towards him, he saw another outrageously dressed woman. She, too, wore vivid lip paint and a low-cut black blouse that showed off her ample cleavage. Her short skirt revealed lithe legs that gave no hint of ever doing knee walking. When she stopped and gazed boldly at Jonathan, he practically stopped breathing. She was on the verge of speaking, when a police wagon barreled around the corner and jerked to a stop between the two women.

Several men dressed in black jumped out, grabbed both women, leering and pinching as they hauled the women shrieking and kicking into the wagon. Before Jonathan had time to protest, the policemen slammed the doors shut, the driver cracked his whip, and off they went. One of the officers remained behind, writing some notes in a little black book that he pulled from his pocket.

"Excuse me, sir," said Jonathan, "I'd like to report a robbery."

"That's not my department," replied the policeman, without even glancing up from his notebook.

Jonathan was stymied. Glancing at the name tag under the man's badge, Jonathan asked, "What's your department, ah, Officer Stuart?"

"Immorals," said the man.

"Beg your pardon?"

"Immorals Department. At our Department we're concerned with immoral behavior."

"Surely robbery is immoral." Getting no further response, Jonathan asked, "Why were those women arrested?"

Officer Stuart finally looked up from his notations and saw

Jonathan's perplexed look. "Couldn't you tell by their clothes? Those women were guilty of giving men sexual favors in exchange for cash. It would have been much better for them if they had bartered for those favors instead."

"Barter? What do you mean by 'barter'?" asked Jonathan, who was less concerned about his own troubles at the moment and increasingly curious about those women.

"I mean," said the policeman, emphasizing every single word, "those women should have entertained their associates after receiving dinner, drinks, dancing, and a theater ticket instead of cash. It's better for community business and perfectly legal."

This confused Jonathan even more. "So cash must never be used for sexual favors?"

"There are exceptions, of course. For example, cash may be paid for the activity if it is filmed and shown to all the people in town. Then it's a public, not private, event and permitted. Instead of getting arrested, the participants may even become celebrities and earn a fortune from a sell-out audience."

"So it's the trading of cash for purely private sexual activity that's immoral?" asked Jonathan.

"There are exceptions for private cash transactions, too, especially when the women wear nicer clothing than those streetwalkers," said Officer Stuart with disdain. "Short-term deals, for an hour or overnight, are illegal. But for a permanent, lifetime contract between a couple, cash may be used. In fact, parents sometimes encourage their children to make such deals. Aspirants to nobility have often been revered for this kind of behavior. Properly done, such contracts provide legitimate means for improving social status and security."

The policeman finished making his notes and reached into a bag. He pulled out a stoneonastick and some nails. "Mind giving me a hand over here?"

"Sure," said Jonathan uncomfortably. He tried to reconcile these strange moral standards.

Officer Stuart turned and walked to a store nearby. He took hold of some loose boards piled on the sidewalk and motioned to Jonathan. "Here, hold this end up. I need to board up the windows of this shop."

"Why are you boarding up this shop?"

"The shop is closed," he said in a voice muffled from holding the nails in his mouth. "The owner was found guilty of selling obscene pictures and got sent to the zoo."

"What's an obscene picture?" asked Jonathan, naively.

"Well, an obscene picture is of some foul and disgusting activity."

"Was the shopkeeper doing this 'disgusting' activity?"

"No, he was just selling the pictures."

Jonathan thought about this carefully as the man finished nailing the top board across the door. "So selling pictures of an obscene act makes one guilty of the act?"

Now it was the policeman's turn to stop and deliberate. "Well, in a way, yes. People who sell such pictures are guilty of promoting the activity. Consumers are easily influenced, you know."

Jonathan struck his palm against his forehead. "I get it! This must have been the newspaper office. You have arrested the news photographers for taking pictures of warfare and killing! But are your newspapers guilty of promoting warfare and killing just because they print and sell the pictures?"

"No, no. Ouch!" exclaimed the officer, shaking his thumb in pain and letting fly a string of violent curses. He had missed a nail and struck his thumb by mistake. Officer Stuart glanced around self-consciously to see who might have heard him swearing. Picking up his tools, he started again. "Obscenity is sexual activity—only performed by perverts! Decent folk condemn such behavior. On the other hand," said the man, "warfare and killing are things that decent people and perverts may all read about and do together. In fact, graphic reporting of these things can earn journalistic awards."

As soon as the last board had been securely hammered in place, Officer Stuart picked up his tools and walked away. Jonathan looked down at his cat Mices. "Guess he's too busy with immorality to help me with a mere robbery."

CHAPTER 34

MERRYBERRIES

As Jonathan wondered where to go next, a rotund, sloppily dressed woman approached him cautiously. The woman's greasy unkempt hair repulsed him, and she smelled like a putrid swamp. Mices darted away. "Psst! Do you want to feel good?" whispered the woman nervously. Jonathan recoiled in disgust. She repeated in a strained voice, "Do you want to feel good?"

After the policeman's description of immorality, Jonathan felt unsure of what to say. However, he thought that this repulsive woman could not be trying to sell sexual favors. So Jonathan, being an honest, sensible kid, answered truthfully, "Doesn't everyone want to feel good?"

"Come with me," said the woman, gripping his arm firmly. She led him down an alley and through a dingy, darkened doorway. Jonathan remembered the robbery and tried to hang back—holding his breath to shield himself from her stench. Before he could protest, the woman closed the door behind him and locked it. She motioned to Jonathan to sit at the table. From her bag, she pulled out a small case of thick cigars. Selecting one, she bit the end, lit the other end with a match, and drew a long, satisfying puff.

Jonathan shifted uncomfortably in his seat and asked, "What do you want?"

She exhaled a plume of smoke explosively and said gruffly, "You want—merryberries?"

"What are merryberries?" asked Jonathan.

The woman's eyes narrowed suspiciously. "You don't know what merryberries are?"

"No," said Jonathan, starting to get up from his chair, "and I really don't think I'm interested, thank you."

The woman ordered him to sit down and he reluctantly complied. After puffing on her cigar and scrutinizing him closely, she said, "Say, you're not from around here, are you?"

Jonathan paused, worrying that she guessed he was a new newcomer. But before he could reply, the woman yelled, "False alarm! Come on out, Doobie."

A hidden door suddenly opened behind a tall, narrow mirror and a uniformed police officer came bounding through. "How do you do?" said the policeman, thrusting his hand out for Jonathan to shake. "I'm Doobie and this is my partner, Mary Jane. Sorry to inconvenience you but we're undercover agents rooting out the merryberry trade." Turning to Mary Jane he added, "I'm starved. Let's make it up to this young fella with a little refreshment."

From the cupboards in the room, they began pulling boxes, packages, bottles, and jars of every size and shape. Food! Jonathan breathed a sigh of relief and his mouth watered at the sight of a feast. The two began to help themselves to the goodies scattered on the table. There were pastries of all types—fresh bread, butter and jam, slices of cheese, chocolate confections, and other tasty delights. Doobie grabbed a hunk of biscuit and dabbed butter and jam thickly on top with his fingers. "Dig in, kid," he said through mouthfuls of food. He waved his hand over the table, "No politicafes for the Merryberry Squad, right Mary Jane?" She could only nod, her fat cheeks bulging from the bon bon in her mouth.

Jonathan took a slice of bread with jam and ate hungrily. Pausing to make conversation, he asked again, "What are merryberries?"

Mary Jane poured a cup of coffee and heaped three spoonfuls of sugar into it. As she stirred some thick cream into the cup, she replied, "You really don't know? Well, merryberries are an illegal fruit. If you had tried to buy merryberries from me, then you would have gone to the zoo for ten or twenty years."

Jonathan's loud gulp could be heard across the room. He had narrowly escaped the zoo! Mary Jane and Doobie caught a look at each other's face for a moment and instantly burst out laughing.

"But what's so bad about merryberries?" demanded Jonathan. "Does it make people sick? Or violent?"

"Worse than that," said Doobie as he used his sleeve to wipe the smears of jam and butter from his cheeks. "Merryberries make people feel good. They just sit quietly and dream."

"Disgusting," added Mary Jane as she lit up a thick stogie and handed it to Doobie. Taking a buttery biscuit and spreading generous layers of cream cheese on top, she muttered, "It's an escape from reality."

"Yeah," said Doobie, adjusting his gun belt more comfortably and mumbling through another mouthful of biscuit. Jonathan had never seen anyone cram food into his mouth so fast. "Young people nowadays just don't take responsibility for their lives. So when they turn to merryberries as an escape, we bring 'em back to reality. We arrest 'em and lock 'em behind bars."

"Is that better for them?" asked Jonathan, discreetly offering Doobie a napkin.

"Sure," responded Mary Jane. "Wanna shot of whiskey, Doobie?" Doobie grinned and thrust a greasy glass toward her. She filled it to the brim with brown fluid from an unlabelled jug. Returning to Jonathan's original question, she replied, "You see, merryberries are addictive."

"What do you mean?"

"It means you always want to have more. You feel like you must have it to continue living."

Jonathan considered this. "You mean like food?" he said, barely audible over the huge belch that exploded from Doobie.

Doobie chuckled contentedly as he downed his second shot of booze and puffed deeply on his cigar. "No, no. Merryberries have no nutritional value and may even be unhealthy. Hand me the ashtray will you, Mary Jane?"

"And if merryberries are unhealthy," said Mary Jane, as she stirred her coffee with a stick of candy, "then we'd all have to pay for the treatment of those sorry derelicts, no matter how foolish their behavior and habits. Uncontrolled merryberry eaters would be a burden on all of us."

Jonathan blurted out, "If people harm themselves, why should you pay for their folly?"

"It's the only humane thing to do," said Doobie, now a bit tipsy. His hands were swinging and jabbing in the air with every thought that came to mind. "We solve human problems. The Lords gotta pay for a lot of problems, ya know, like our salaries and the big zoos. And don't forget, last year, the Council of Lords had to help the tobacco and sugar farmers get through a bad year. Gotta feed the people, don't ya know? Taxes solve these problems and plenty more. Taxes care for people who become ill. It's the only decent, civilized thing to do. Pass the whiskey, Mary Jane."

Mary Jane passed him the jug and nodded in agreement. She lit a new cigar from her packet by touching it to the stub of her previous smoke. Doobie was on a roll. "Because we gotta help everyone, we gotta control what everyone does."

"We?" questioned Jonathan.

"Eek!" belched Doobie. "Excuse me!" He took a pill bottle from his shirt pocket. "When I say 'we' I don't mean you and me personally. I mean that the Lords decide for us what is good behavior and who must pay for bad behavior. In fact, it's good behavior to pay for bad behavior. Does that make sense, Mary Jane? Anyway, the Lords don't make mistakes on these decisions like the rest of us would." Doobie stopped to down a couple of little red pills. His words were beginning to slur. "Funny how I always say 'we' when talking about them. Mary Jane, would you like a couple of these to calm your nerves?"

"Thanks, but no thanks," she said graciously. She slipped a delicate metal box across to him adding, "My pretty pink pacifiers work a lot faster. I can hardly start the day without my coffee and one of these. Here, try one if you like. It's the latest in prescribed chemistry."

Jonathan reflected on the politicians he had met so far. "Are the Lords wise enough to show people correct behavior?"

"Somebody has to!" bellowed Doobie, as he wobbled slightly in his chair. He took another slug of whiskey to wash down a mouth filled with cakes and pink pills and glared at Jonathan. "If people don't behave correctly, we'll certainly teach the bums responsibility when they get to the zoo!" Doobie began to plead with the others to join him in a round of drinks.

"No, thank you," said Jonathan. "What do you mean by 'responsibility'?"

Mary Jane moved to pour a little whiskey into her coffee before adding still more sugar and cream. "I don't know how to...well, Doobie, you explain it."

"Hmmm. Let me think." Doobie tilted his chair back and puffed on his cigar. He might have looked wise except that he almost lost his balance. Recovering, he said, "Responsibility must be accepting the consequences of your own actions. Yes, that's it! It's the only way to grow, you know, to learn." The smoke around Doobie thickened as he puffed faster, trying to think hard about responsibility.

"No, no," interrupted Mary Jane. "That's too selfish. Responsibility is taking charge of others. You know—when we keep them from harm, when we protect them from themselves."

Jonathan asked, "Which is more selfish? To take care of yourself or to take charge of others?"

"There's only one way to figure this out," declared Doobie. He stood bolt upright from his chair, knocking it to the floor. "Let's take him to the Grand Inquirer. If anyone can explain responsibility, he can!"

CHAPTER 35

THE GRAND INQUIRER

he shadows had lengthened into late afternoon. Jonathan and his two acquaintances, Mary Jane and Doobie, emerged from the alley. Somewhere on the street, Mices rejoined him as they walked to a grassy park. People entered the park from all directions, some on foot and some on knees, and gathered around a hillock in the center.

"Good," said Mary Jane, "we're early. Soon this place will be filled with followers who have come to hear the Grand Inquirer's truth. All your questions will be answered." They sat down on a mound of grass. Doobie, overcome by food and whiskey, promptly fell back and passed out. Mary Jane grew quiet. Families settled under the trees and all waited expectantly.

Jonathan overheard a man behind him say, "Wonderful! I didn't expect the Grand Inquirer today."

His companion replied, "Nobody expects the Grand Inquirer, whose chief elements of proof are..."

At that instant a tall, gaunt figure clad completely in black strode rapidly into the middle of the gathering. His eyes slowly swept the faces gazing up at him. The murmuring of the crowd stopped and all grew silent.

The man's hard voice seemed to rise from the very ground and penetrated Jonathan's whole body. "Peace is war! Wisdom is ignorance! Freedom is slavery!"

Jonathan glanced around at the silent awestruck crowd. The Grand Inquirer had mesmerized his audience. But young Jonathan blurted, "Why do you say 'freedom is slavery'?"

Stunned by Jonathan's brashness, Mary Jane chided him in a whisper, "I said you'll have your questions answered—I didn't say you could ask him questions."

The Grand Inquirer fixed a piercing look on his young examiner. No one before had the effrontery to challenge him. The light rustle of wind in the leaves made the only sound in that park. Then the Grand Inquirer growled, half at Jonathan, half at the crowd, "Freedom is the greatest of all burdens that mankind can bear." Roaring at the top of his voice, the man raised his arms and crossed his wrists high above his head, "Freedom is the heaviest of chains!"

"Why?" persisted Jonathan, finally feeling the courage of an outsider who doesn't worry much about what others might think of him.

The Grand Inquirer moved directly in front of Jonathan and spoke gravely, "Freedom is a monumental weight on the shoulders of men and women because it requires the use of mind and will." With a roar of pain and horror, the Grand Inquirer warned, "Free will would make you all fully responsible for your own actions!" The crowd shuddered at his words; some clapped their hands over their ears in fright.

"What do you mean 'responsible'?" asked Jonathan in an unwavering voice.

The Inquirer retreated a step and his face softened in a kindly expression. He reached down to pluck a sprig growing near his foot. "My beloved brothers and sisters, you may not realize the dangers of which I speak. Close your eyes and imagine the life of this tiny plant." His voice grew soft and caressed the crowd.

Everyone, except Jonathan, pressed his or her eyes tightly closed and concentrated. Hypnotically, the Grand Inquirer began to describe a picture to the assembly. "This little plant is but a frail bit of shrubbery, rooted in soil and fixed upon the earth. It is not responsible for its actions. All of its actions are preset. Ah, the bliss of a shrub!

"Now, beloved, imagine an animal. A cute, busy little mouse scurrying to find its food among the plants. This furry creature is not responsible for its actions. All that a mouse does is predetermined by nature. Ah, nature. Happy animal! Neither plant nor animal suffers any burden of the will because neither faces choice. They can never be wrong!"

A few in the crowd murmured, "Yes, Grand Inquirer, yes, yes, so it is."

This charismatic leader straightened, suddenly taller, and continued, "Open your eyes and look around you! A human being, one who succumbs to values and choices, can be wrong I tell you! Wrong values and choices can hurt you and others. Even the knowledge of choice will cause suffering. That suffering is responsibility."

The people shuddered and huddled closer together. A boy seated next to Jonathan cried out suddenly, "Oh please, master. How can we avoid this fate?"

"Tell us how to rid ourselves of this terrible burden," pleaded another.

"It will not be easy, but together we can conquer this terrifying threat." Then he spoke in a voice so soft that Jonathan had to lean forward to catch his words. "Trust me. I will make the decisions for you. You are then relieved of all the guilt and responsibility that freedom brings. As decision maker, I will take all the suffering upon myself."

Then the Inquirer flung his arms high and shouted, "Now go forth, every one of you. Comb the streets and alleys, knock on every door. Get out the vote as I have instructed you! Victory is at hand for me, your decision maker on the Council of Lords!" And the crowd shouted their approval, rose as one and scrambled away in all directions. They pushed and shoved, eager to be the first to hit the streets.

Only Jonathan and the Grand Inquirer were left—and Doobie, gently snoring in the grass. Jonathan sat in disbelief. He watched the mad dash of the group, then he peered at the face of the man in black. The Inquirer looked past Jonathan, as if seeing some distant vision. Jonathan broke the eerie silence with one more question. "What virtue is there in turning all decisions over to you?"

"None," replied the Inquirer with a contemptuous sneer. "Virtue can only exist if there is freedom of choice. My flock prefers serenity to virtue. As for you, little one with too many questions, what do you prefer? Let me make your choices, too. Then your questions won't matter."

Speechless, Jonathan walked away from the empty park. The Grand Inquirer's laughter rang out behind him.

CHAPTER 36

LOSER LAW

onathan hoped it was time to rendezvous with Alisa. He frequently thought of her. Moreover, he looked forward to telling her about his experiences. In anticipation, his footsteps quicken on the pavement.

As he retraced his path, Jonathan heard shouting and whooping from a great throng of people. In a vacant lot across from BLOCK A, BLOCK B, and BLOCK C, a raised, square platform had been erected and was surrounded by ropes. An excited, shouting crowd pressed close to the perimeter. He noticed that everyone in the crowd was wearing a wide belt or brace on their backs.

In the middle of the platform, a man was yelling at the top of his lungs. "In this corner—weighing 256 pounds—five months the undefeated champion of the Workers' International Competition—the Terrible Tiger— Karl 'the Masher' Marlow!" The crowd went wild.

Off to one side, a man with a scar on his face sat at a rickety table, deftly shuffling through a pile of papers and stacks of money. The man looked up at Jonathan and barked, "Place your bet, sonny. Only a few seconds before the next round."

An eager old woman, elbowed Jonathan aside and slapped a handful of bills on the table. "Fifty on the champ, quick!" she demanded.

"Okay, lady," said the clerk. He stamped a ticket, tore the stub from a ledger, and handed it to her.

The announcer crossed the platform calling out, "And in the far corner—the challenger—weighing in at 270 pounds of pure muscle—the knuckle-crunching stevedore..."

Turning to the man at the table, Jonathan asked, "Some trouble going on? Is there gonna be a fight?"

"A fight for sure, but hardly any trouble," said the man with a grin. "Never had it so good." The bell clanged and the man shouted to the crowd, "Bets closed!" Both men leaped forward, swinging punches and ducking each other's blows.

"Listen, sonny, there's nothin' to get nervous about," consoled the clerk. "The winner and the loser both take home a bundle of cash."

One of the fighters suddenly hit the floor, knocked on his back by a solid punch. The crowd roared with enthusiasm while the clerk counted money into an iron box.

"Both win a prize?" asked Jonathan.

"...five hundred, six hundred...sure," said the man, stopping the count momentarily. "This is the most popular fight on the island. Sometimes the loser makes out better than the winner...seven hundred, eight hundred..."

Jonathan's eyes widened. "Anyone can get rich by losing?"

"Not everyone. You gotta have a good job to lose before you can take on the champ."

"I don't get it," said Jonathan. "Why would a worker risk his job to get smashed by the champ?" The bell ended another round and the crowd quieted down.

"...nine hundred, a thousand. That's the whole idea. Haven't you ever heard of the Loser Law?" asked the man, tapping the money into neat stacks. "The Loser Law eliminates the risk. The loser doesn't worry about a thing—paycheck, doctor bills, nothin'."

"Why not?" asked Jonathan.

"After a fight, the loser never works again and his employer pays everything."

Jonathan craned his neck over the crowd and saw one man slumped in the corner getting his face mopped by a ring assistant. "What's the employer have to do with this fight?"

"Nothing, really," said the man. "The worker claims he got injured on the job and can't go back to work, right?"

"Okay," replied Jonathan, trying hard to follow. "You mean the loser might lie in order to get the money?"

"It's been known to happen," said the man with a sly wink. "Don't get me wrong, not all workers will lie to get a few years on the gravy train.

But the Loser Law rewards those who do. So every day we're getting more players. It's an attractive arrangement. No one has disproven a claim in forty years."

Jonathan finally understood why everyone was wearing those special belts and braces. "What's the Council do about it?"

The man chuckled, "They'll support us on anything—and we're loyal on Election Day."

"Police!" shouted someone in the crowd. Dozens dropped to their knees. The clerk quickly clapped his moneybox shut, folded up the table, and whistled nonchalantly.

Jonathan scanned the street for signs of the police. Seeing Officer Stuart and other policemen approach the ring, Jonathan asked, "What's the matter? Is the fight illegal?"

"Heavens no," replied the man coolly. "The police enjoy a good match as much as the next guy. It's free-lance gambling that's illegal. The Council of Lords says that games of chance are immoral—except at the Special Interest Carnival where they take a cut of the winnings. As for Tweed, well, she thinks it's better if we save our bets for the election."

Just then the bell rang out and the crowd cheered. Jonathan felt a tap on his shoulder and turned. It was Alisa. She smiled and said, "Where's your cat?"

CHAPTER 37

THE DEMOCRACY GANG

onathan didn't have time to say hello. Someone screamed, "It's them! The Democracy Gang! Run for cover!"

"Run, run," shouted a kid, who sprinted past Jonathan.

Alisa's face lost its color. "We've got to get out of here—fast!"

First to disappear were the police. The crowd scattered in all directions—many of them shedding their back braces to run faster. Three whole families, with children in tow, raced down the stairs of BLOCK B and tossed belongings out the windows to friends below. All gathered what they could and dashed up the street.

Moments later the street was nearly empty. Only the slowest, their arms laden with bundles or children, could still be seen heading away from the approaching threat. A structure at the far end of the street burst into flames. Frozen with fear, Jonathan grabbed Alisa's arm demanding, "What's going on? Why's everyone so scared?"

Tugging wildly against his grip, Alisa yanked Jonathan to his feet and cried out, "It's the Democracy Gang! We've gotta get out of here quick!"

"Why?"

"No time for questions, let's go!" she shouted. But Jonathan refused to budge. Scared to death she cried, "Let's go or they'll get us!"

"Who?"

"The Democracy Gang! They surround anyone they find and they vote on what to do with them. They take their money, lock 'em in a cage, or force 'em to join their gang. There's nothing anyone can do to stop them!"

Jonathan's head was spinning. Where were those ubiquitous police now? "Can't the law protect us from the gang?"

"Look," said Alisa, still wriggling to escape Jonathan's hand, "run now and talk later."

"There's time. Tell me, quick."

She looked over his shoulder. She swallowed hard and spoke frantically. "When the gang first attacked people, the police hauled them into court for their crimes. The gang argued that they were following majority rule, same as the law. Votes decide everything—legality, morality, everything!"

"Were they convicted?" asked Jonathan. By now, the street was completely deserted.

"Would I be running now if they had been? No, the judges ruled three to two in their favor. 'Divine Right of Majorities' they called it. Ever since then the gang has been free to go after anyone they could outnumber."

The senseless rules and ways of the island finally got to Jonathan. "How can people live in a place like this? There must be a way to defend yourself!"

"Without weapons, you can only flee or join another gang with more members."

Jonathan loosened his hold and they both ran. On and on they went, up alleys, through gates, around corners, across plazas. Alisa knew the town as well as she knew the back of her hand.

The two kept running until they were exhausted. Finally, well beyond the streets and houses, they climbed a steep bluff hoping to reach safety high above the town. The last rays of sun died in the West and Jonathan saw fires breaking out in the town below. The sounds of distant screams and shouts occasionally floated up to their perch.

"I can't go any further," gasped Alisa, her long brown hair draped over her shoulders in a tangle. She backed up to a tree, panting to regain her breath. Jonathan sat down exhausted and braced himself against a rock. In her mad run, she had torn her frock and lost her shoes. "I wonder what happened to my folks," she worried.

Jonathan worried, too. He thought about the old couple who had taken such good care of him the night before—and their little grandson, Davy. Every individual seemed helpless in this strange world. "Alisa, too bad you don't have a good Council to keep the peace."

Alisa stared at Jonathan and sat down next to him. "You've got it mixed up," she said. Still trying to catch her breath, she pointed in the direction of the riots. "For as long as anyone can remember, people have learned to take from each other by force. Who do you suppose taught them?"

Jonathan frowned and answered, "You mean someone taught them to use force against each other?"

"Most of us learned it by example every day."

"Why didn't the Council of Lords stop them?" said Jonathan.

"The Council *is* force," said Alisa, emphatically, "and most of the time it's used against people instead of protecting people." She saw Jonathan's blank look. He obviously didn't have the slightest idea of what she was talking about. She pushed her forefinger into his chest and said, "Listen, when you want something from another person, how do you get it?"

Still feeling his bruise from the robber, Jonathan responded, "You mean, without a gun?"

"Yeah."

"Well, I could try to persuade them," answered Jonathan.

"Right. Or?"

"Or-or, I could pay them?"

"Yes, that's a kind of persuasion. How else?"

"Hmmm. Go to the Council of Lords for a law?"

"Exactly," said Alisa. "With government you don't have to persuade people. If you get the Council of Lords on your side, either by votes or bribery, then you can force others to do what you want. When someone else offers the Council more, then he can force you to do whatever he wants. And the Lords are always winners."

"But I thought government encouraged cooperation," said Jonathan.

"Hardly! Who needs cooperation when you can use force," responded Alisa. "Anyone with power can win whatever they want—and the rest have to put up with it. It's legal, but the losers remain unconvinced, bitter, and hostile."

Alisa directed Jonathan's gaze to the fires below. "Look at the riot down there," she said. "Society is torn apart by this constant struggle for power. All over the island, groups that lose too many votes eventually explode in frustration."

She sat still for a long time. A tear began to trickle down her cheek. "My dad and I have arranged a special place to meet when this happens. But I'll wait until the fires die down."

Jonathan sat quietly a long time, bewildered by these two long days since the storm. By the time he looked back at Alisa, she had fallen into a deep sleep. He was very impressed with her—everything about her. As he made himself comfortable, he thought, "She's no simple Phoebe Simon."

CHAPTER 38

VULTURES, BEGGARS, CON MEN, AND KINGS

ext morning, the first rays of light awakened Jonathan. He heard purring; Mices was enjoying a long stretch—digging his claws in the soil. Jonathan rubbed his eyes and looked wearily around. Aside from a few columns of smoke, the town seemed quiet again. Hungrily he searched his pockets and found a couple remaining slices of bread. He ate one and, trying not to wake Alisa, gently placed a slice under her hand. But she stirred and sat up.

"I want to take a look from the top of this mountain," he told her. She agreed and they began heading up the steep slope together. Soon the path gave way to rocks that required hand over hand climbing and hauling, using any protruding branch or root. Well ahead of Alisa, but behind Mices, Jonathan arrived at an outcropping near the top. He surveyed the town far below. The summit was near, so he continued up an incline and through a stand of stunted and twisted trees.

"People!" he said to himself, exasperated. "Constantly pushing each other around. Threatening each other. Arresting each other. Robbing and harming each other."

Eventually, the trees thinned out to a few bushes, and then, a pile of large boulders. A faint, full moon could still be seen fading in the dawn, slipping closer to the horizon. The air was cool and pleasant as he trudged along. On the peak was a single scraggly tree with a big, ugly black vulture perched on a bare limb. "Oh no," groaned Jonathan, who had hoped for a more lonely spot. "Just my luck. I leave behind a valley of vultures in order to find peace and what do I find? A real vulture!"

"I am a condor!" echoed a deep, gruff voice.

Jonathan froze. Mices jumped, then arched his back and began to hiss. Jonathan's eyes, wider than the moon, moved slowly, surveying the area. His heart pounded fast in his ears. Lips trembling, he asked, "Who said that?"

"Who said that?" repeated the voice. It seemed to come from that isolated tree.

Jonathan eyed the vulture-like bird. Neither moved. He spoke, "You talk? Nah, vultures can't talk!"

Mustering his courage and taking a deep breath, Jonathan slowly approached the tree. The bird didn't move a feather, though Jonathan had the distinct feeling of being under its gaze.

Again Jonathan spoke, trying to keep his voice steady, "You talk?"

"Of course?" replied the condor arrogantly. "I am a condor, the largest member of the proud vulture family." Jonathan's knees buckled and he nearly fell. He caught himself and lowered into a crouch before the tree. "You—you, can speak?"

"Ahem," puffed the bird. "Can you? You don't seem to know what you're saying half the time. Just mimicking, I suppose." The bird swiveled his head slightly and said, in an accusing tone, "What did you mean when you said you left a valley of vultures?"

"I-I-I'm sorry. I didn't mean to insult you," sputtered Jonathan, feeling a little silly to be talking with a bird. "All those people down there were so cruel and brutal to each other. It's just a figure of speech about vultures and such. The people reminded me of, well, of..."

"Vultures?" The bird expanded the ruff of feathers below his naked head. Jonathan nodded meekly.

Alisa emerged from the trees and the sight of the exchange took her breath away. "He exists!" she exclaimed. She hastened to Jonathan's side and grasped his arm whispering, "The great Bard really exists! I thought it was only a myth. I never imagined—and so big and ugly!"

The condor grunted and flapped his great wings before settling back on his branch. "Thank you for the kind introduction, Alisa."

Seeing her surprise at hearing her name, the Bard responded, "You knew of me. Why shouldn't I know of you and your friend, Jonathan?"

Alisa and Jonathan looked at the condor, awestruck.

"I've watched you both for some time now, especially Jonathan's harrowing trial at sea," said the Bard. "You're brave and clever, young man, but easily fooled. Alisa is more insightful, more likely to trust actions than words."

"I don't understand," said Jonathan.

"To you, this land is all vultures. Hmph! If that was true, then this would be a far better island than it is." The bird raised its ugly, naked head proudly. "You have come to an island of many creatures—vultures, beggars, con men, and kings. But you don't recognize who is worthy because titles and words deceive you. You have fallen for the oldest of tricks and hold evil in high esteem."

Jonathan defended himself. "There's no trick. Vultures, beggars, and so forth are easy to understand. Where I come from, vultures pick the bones of the dead. That's disgusting!" Jonathan's nose wrinkled in emphasis. "Beggars are simple and innocent. Con men are clever and funny—sort of mischievous."

"As for kings and royalty," added Jonathan quickly, his eye's dancing with a glint of excitement, "well, I've never met any in real life, but I've read that they live in beautiful palaces and wear gorgeous clothes. Everyone wants to be like them. Kings and their ministers rule the land and serve to protect all their subjects. That's no trick."

"No trick?" repeated the Bard, amused. "Consider the vulture. Of the four, the vulture is the only one of true nobility. Only the vulture does anything worthwhile."

The great black bird stretched his neck again and glared at Jonathan. "Whenever a mouse dies behind the barn, I clean up. Whenever a horse dies in the field, I clean up. Whenever a poor man dies in the woods, I clean up. I get a meal and everyone is better off. No one ever used a gun or a cage to get me to do my job. Do I get any thanks? No. My services are considered dirty and foul. So the 'ugly' vulture must live with verbal abuse and no appreciation.

"Then there are the beggars," continued the condor. "They don't produce. They don't help anyone, except themselves. But they do no harm either. They keep themselves from dying in the woods, of course. And it can be said that they provide a sense of well-being to their benefactors. So they are tolerated.

"Con men are the most cunning and have earned a high place in poetry and legend. They practice deceit and cheat others with the words they weave. Con men perform no useful service, except to teach distrust and the art of fraud."

Rearing up and throwing his huge wings open, the condor sighed deeply. A faint smell of carrion perfumed the morning air. "The lowest are royalty. Kings need not beg nor deceive; though they often do both. Like robbers, they steal the product of others with the brute force at their command. They produce nothing, yet they control everything. And you, my naive traveler, revere this 'royalty' while you scorn the vulture? If you saw an ancient monument," observed the Bard, "you would say that the king was great because his name was inscribed at the top. Yet, you give no thought to all the carcasses that my kind had to clean up while the monument was being built."

Jonathan spoke up, "True, in the past some kings were villains. But now voters elect their leaders to a Council of Lords. They're different because—well, because they're elected."

"Elected Lords different? Ha!" cried the condor harshly. "Children are still raised on fantasies about royalty and, when they grow up, royalty is still what they expect. Your elected Lords are nothing more than four-year kings and two-year princes. Indeed, they combine beggars, con men, and royalty all rolled into one! They beg or scheme for contributions and votes; they flatter and deceive at every opportunity; they prance around the island as rulers. And, when they succeed in their exploits, those of us who truly produce and serve get less and less."

Jonathan fell silent. He gazed back down to the valley and nodded his head in resignation. "I'd like to see a place where it isn't like that. Could there be such a place?"

Lifting his great wings, the condor sprang from the tree and landed with a resounding thud next to Jonathan and Alisa. They jumped back, surprised at the great size of the bird. The Bard leaned over them, almost twice their height, with a gigantic wingspan.

"You would like to see a place where people are free? Where force is used only for protection? You would like to visit a land where officials are governed by the same rules of behavior as everyone else?"

"Oh yes!" said Jonathan eagerly.

The Bard studied them both carefully. The bird's huge eyes bore right through Jonathan, reading him for signs of sincerity. Then he declared, "Jonathan, climb on my back." The bird turned slightly and lowered his broad stiff tail feathers to the ground.

Jonathan's curiosity overcame his fear. He stepped on a notch in the tree and carefully reached out to pull himself up to the soft hollow between the bird's wings. Then he looked expectantly to Alisa.

"I can't leave," she said to them both. "My family is looking for me. I want to go with you sometime, but not now."

Jonathan blushed. With a big smile, he quipped, "I still haven't had that free lunch."

No sooner had Jonathan put his arms around the bird's thick neck than he felt tension in the muscles. The condor leaped awkwardly along the ground in great strides. He felt a lurch and they floated into the rising breeze. Looking back, Jonathan could see Alisa waving, with Mices at her feet.

Sailing high above the island, with the wind beating against his face, Jonathan felt exuberant. Except for missing a few friends, he left the island gladly. The mountains disappeared beneath the clouds and the condor soared straight toward the brilliant rays of the rising sun. A vast ocean of clouds and water stretched ahead and Jonathan wondered, "Where?"

CHAPTER 39

TERRA LIBERTAS

slight headwind blew steadily across Jonathan's face. Time stretched into hours, and the rhythmic motion of the condor's flight made Jonathan drowsy. He dreamed. He was running down a narrow street pursued by the shadowy figures of guards and their unleashed dogs. "Stop, you scalawag—you new newcomer!" they shouted. Terror gripped him, as he desperately pumped his legs harder and harder. One figure loomed out in front of the others—Lady Tweed. He heard her breathing down his neck as she lunged with fat fingers to grab him.

A sharp bump woke Jonathan with a start. "What?" murmured Jonathan, still clutching handfuls of the bird's thick feathers.

They had landed on a beach that looked familiar. The Bard issued instructions. "Follow this strand along the shoreline. Continue a mile or so north and you'll find your bearings." Thick bunches of salt grass waved gently over long, golden sand dunes. The ocean looked gray and cold where it lapped the shore. He climbed gingerly off the back of the bird.

Suddenly, Jonathan realized where he was. "I'm home!" he shouted with joy. He started to run up the sandy slopes of the beach then halted and turned again to the condor. "But, you said you were taking me to a place where things are done right," said Jonathan.

"I have," said the Bard.

"That's not the way it is here," argued Jonathan.

"Not yet, maybe, but it will be when you make it so. Anywhere, even Corrumpo, can be a paradise when the inhabitants are truly free."

"Corrumpo?" gasped Jonathan. "Most believe they're free enough. Lady Tweed told them as much. And the rest are afraid of freedom, so eager are they to give themselves to the Grand Inquirer."

"Mere words!" said the Bard. "The test of freedom comes with action."

Jonathan felt very young. He pulled a reed from the ground and started poking the sand thoughtfully. "What should things be like? I've seen many problems—but what are the solutions?"

The condor let Jonathan's question hover between them while preening his feathers. When the feathers lay clean and smooth, the condor looked out to sea saying, "You're looking for a vision of the future?"

"I suppose so," said Jonathan.

"That's a problem. Rulers always have a vision and force others into it. Remember, rulers have no right to do anything that you have no right to do on your own. If you shouldn't do it, you shouldn't ask others to do it for you."

"But isn't a vision good for knowing where you're headed?"

"For yourself, but not to impose on others." The Bard turned to face Jonathan again, his talons clenching and digging the sand. "In a free land, you place confidence in virtue and discovery. Thousands of creatures seeking their own goals, each striving, will create a far better world than you can possibly imagine for them. Look to the means first, noble ends will follow. Free people find unexpected solutions and those who are not free find unexpected problems."

With skepticism Jonathan groaned, "But no one will listen to me."

"Whether others listen or not, you gain strength by speaking and acting. Those who listen will take courage from you." The condor turned toward the sea readying to leave.

Jonathan yelled, "Wait! Will I see my friends again?"

"When you have prepared your paradise, I'll bring her to see it."

Jonathan watched the great bird gather himself and launch his huge body into the wind. Moments later he disappeared among the clouds.

Jonathan began walking. He did not remember much about that walk except the steady crunch of sand beneath his feet and the gusts of wind on his body. Jonathan recognized a rocky channel that marked the entrance to his village. Soon, he was nearing a house and store at the harbor's edge—his home.

Jonathan's lean, sad-faced father stood coiling rope on the front porch. His eyes widened when he saw his son coming up the path. "Jon," cried his father. "Jon-boy, where've you been?" His voice breaking, he shouted to his wife who was busy cleaning inside. "Rita, look—Jon's back!"

"What's all the ruckus about?" asked Jonathan's mother, looking a little more careworn than he remembered. She came out on the porch and screamed with delight at the sight of her son. Instantly she gathered Jonathan into her arms and hugged him a long time. Then, pushing him back and looking him over at arm's length, she brushed her sleeve across her eyes to stop a flood of joyful tears. "Just where have you been young man? Are you hungry?" Then she said to her husband excitedly, "Stoke the fire, Hubert, and put on the kettle!"

They shared a festive reunion and Jonathan recounted his adventure, occasionally making rough drawings to describe what had transpired. His parents smiled and shook their heads in a mixture of disbelief and happiness. After he had eaten one last slice of his mother's warm pie, he sighed and sat back in his chair. The old store and their living quarters in

the back room glowed in the light of the fireplace. "Son, you seem older," said his father. He looked hard at Jonathan and added jokingly, "Are you sailing again soon?"

"No, Dad," said Jonathan, "I'm here to stay. There's plenty of work to do."

EPILOGUE

r. Gullible, a wise man many years my senior, gave me far more than a story of adventure. During many months of discourse he provided me with an outline of his intriguing philosophy of life. Over the years it guided him to fruitful activity in his homeland. That is yet another story. Nevertheless, I leave you with words from the conclusion of his journal.

My philosophy is based on the principle of self-ownership. You own your life. To deny this is to imply that another person has a higher claim on your life than you do. No other person, or group of persons, owns your life nor do you own the lives of others.

You exist in time: future, present, and past. This is manifest in life, liberty, and the product of your life and liberty. The exercise of choices over life and liberty is your prosperity. To lose your life is to lose your future. To lose your liberty is to lose your present. And to lose the product of your life and liberty is to lose the portion of your past that produced it.

A product of your life and liberty is your property. Property is the fruit of your labor, the product of your time, energy, and talents. It is that part of nature that you turn to valuable use. And it is the property of others that is given to you by voluntary exchange and mutual consent. Two people who exchange property voluntarily are both better off or they wouldn't do it. Only they may rightfully make that decision for themselves.

At times some people use force or fraud to take from others without willful, voluntary consent. Normally, the initiation of force to take life is murder, to take liberty is slavery, and to take property is theft. It is the same whether these actions are done by one person acting alone, by the many acting against a few, or even by officials with fine hats and titles.

You have the right to protect your own life, liberty, and justly acquired property from the forceful aggression of others. So you may rightfully ask others to help protect you. But you do not have a right to initiate force against the life, liberty, or property of others. Thus, you have no right to designate some person to initiate force against others on your behalf.

You have a right to seek leaders for yourself, but you have no right to impose rulers on others. No matter how officials are selected, they are only human beings and they have no rights or claims that are higher than those of any other human beings. Regardless of the imaginative labels for their behavior or the numbers of people encouraging them, officials have no right to murder, to enslave, or to steal. You cannot give them any rights that you do not have yourself.

Since you own your life, you are responsible for your life. You do not rent your life from others who demand your obedience. Nor are you a slave to others who demand your sacrifice. You choose your own goals based on your own values. Success and failure are both the necessary incentives to learn and to grow. Your action on behalf of others, or their action on behalf of you, is only virtuous when it is derived from voluntary, mutual consent. For virtue can only exist when there is free choice.

This is the basis of a truly free society. It is not only the most practical and humanitarian foundation for human action, it is also the most ethical.

Problems that arise from the initiation of force by government have a solution. The solution is for people of the world to stop asking officials to initiate force on their behalf. Evil does not arise only from evil people, but also from good people who tolerate the initiation of force as a means to their own ends. In this manner, good people have empowered evil throughout history.

Having confidence in a free society is to focus on the process of discovery in the marketplace of values rather than to focus on some imposed vision or goal. Using governmental force to impose a vision on others is intellectual sloth and typically results in unintended, perverse consequences. Achieving the free society requires courage to think, to talk, and to act—especially when it is easier to do nothing.

—Jonathan Gullible

QUESTIONS ON THE CHAPTERS

2. **Troublemakers:** What is the purpose of work? Are labor saving innovations good or bad? Why? Who is affected? How can such innovations be stopped? What are some examples of this behavior? What ethical issues are involved with the use of force?

3. **A Commons Tragedy:** How do people treat things that belong to everyone? Who really owns the lake and the fish? How would behavior change if the fisherman owned the lake? Who benefits by common ownership? Examples? What ethical issues are involved?

4. **The Food Police:** Why are some farmers paid not to grow crops? What happens to the price and availability of food for consumers? What kinds of dependency arise? Are there real examples of this behavior? What ethical issues are involved in the use of force?

5. **Candles and Coats:** Is it good for people to get free light and heat from the sun? Who objects? Are the objections to imports similar? Why do people object to imports? How do people stop imports of low cost goods? Examples? What ethical issues are there?

6. **The Tall Tax:** Is it proper to use taxes to manipulate behavior? Do people shape their lives to reduce taxes? Are officials more wise and moral than their subjects? Is it unfair for people to be tall? Examples? What ethical issues are there in this story?

7. **Best Laid Plans:** What is the problem with superior ownership, or eminent domain? If an official can use, control, take, or destroy a house that another person builds, then who really owns the house? Is a property tax like rent? Examples? Ethical issues?

8. **Two Zoos:** Should people be forced to pay for a zoo? What reasons could there be for not paying? What happens to people who would refuse to pay such a tax? On which side of the fence are the people who are harming others? Examples? Ethical issues?

9. **Making Money:** Is it good or bad to print money? Who decides? How are people affected differently? Is there a comparison between counterfeiters and official money printers? Who is blamed for rising prices? Examples? What are the ethical issues?

10. **The Dream Machine:** Whose dream really came true? Why? Have Newly Industrialized Economies (NIE) benefited by high wage demands in other places? What is an alternative to legal tender? What is meant by "There ain't no such thing as a free lunch"?

11. **Power Sale:** What are legal and illegal forms of bribery? Can politicians legally bribe voters and vice versa? What are problems associated with bribery? How can Council debt be likened to "taking candy from a baby"? Examples? Ethical issues?

12. **Helter Shelter:** How are different groups of people affected by rent controls, building codes, and zoning? How does market activity punish or reward business practices that are good or bad? How are these reversed by rent controls? Examples? Ethical issues?

13. **Escalating Crimes:** What is meant by an "escalating crime"? What can happen to someone who resists arrest? How are groups of people affected differently by occupational licensing laws? Does the law make or break monopolies? Why? Examples? Ethical issues?

14. **Book Battles:** How can the selection of books be an act of propaganda or censorship? Should people be forced to pay for books they don't like? Can libraries exist without tax funding? How are incentives different for government and private libraries?

15. **Nothing to It:** What problems arise when art is financed by taxes? Is the selection of art elitist? Can officials be objective in funding art? Can art exist without tax funding? How does the type of funding affect behavior? Examples? What ethical issues are involved?

16. **The Special Interest Carnival:** Are the game participants winners? Why are the pavilion operators happy? Should people be required to participate in carnivals like this? How can political "logrolling" be compared to this game? Examples? Ethical issues?

17. **Uncle Samta:** Does Uncle Samta give back as much as he takes? Why don't people complain when he takes things from their homes? Why did officials take over Christmas rituals? How would Christmas behavior be affected? Examples? Ethical issues?

18. **The Tortoise and the Hare Revisited:** What are the differences in government and private mail delivery? Who receives benefits from the granting of monopoly privileges? Can control over mail delivery allow for control over citizens? Ethical issues?

19. **Bored of Digestion:** Are customers satisfied with the politicafes? How is the menu decided? Are truants and cooks treated properly? What would happen if food for the mind were treated as this island treats food for the stomach? Examples? Ethical issues?

20. **"Give Me Your Past or Your Future!":** How are life, liberty, and property relative to time? In what way is a thief the same or different than a tax collector? Why? Are small scale and large scale immorality treated differently? Examples? Ethical issues?

21. **The Bazaar of Governments:** Why does the herdsman trade one of his cows to buy a bull? What are the similarities in the governments that are offered? Are there examples of this behavior in the world? What ethical issues are involved in the use of force?

22. **The World's Oldest Profession:** Are there similarities between some fortunetellers and some economists? What percent of these can accurately predict the future? How can you tell? Do professionals ever put their talents to unworthy use?

23. **Booting Production:** Why are people paid not to produce? Would you take a job that paid you to do nothing? Would you pay others to do nothing? Would you take welfare that paid you to do nothing? Are there examples in the world? Ethical issues?

QUESTIONS ON THE CHAPTERS

24. The Applausometer: Is it logical to determine morality, power, wealth, and rights by the enthusiasm of applause? Is it logical to determine these things by numbers of votes? What is the best basis for determining these? Examples? Ethical issues?

25. True Believer: Why do voters usually vote for incumbents? Are politicians trustworthy? Does one have a right to complain about politics if one does not vote? Is there any parallel between the behavior of abused spouses and abused voters? Ethical issues?

26. According to Need: Would student performance change if bad scores were given high grades and vice versa? Can economic systems be like this? Do schools contradict life in the real world? Would teachers accept the incentives offered to students? Ethics?

27. Wages of Sin: What are reasons that people are arrested for working? Why are people helped or hurt by this? When is it wrong to want work? Do volunteers violate minimum wage laws? Are schools or prisons better for people than the workplace? Ethical issues?

28. New Newcomers: Are border guards responsible for what happens to refugees who are turned away? What is the difference between newcomers and new newcomers? Why? Should young men be required to work for the military? Examples? Ethical issues?

29. Treat or Trick?: Why is bread put into the big basket? Why is the bread supply running low? What solutions are offered to fix the shortage? What is a better solution? How does this affect human behavior? Are there examples in the world? Ethical issues?

30. Whose Brilliant Idea?: Can one own the use of an idea? Do patents assure that inventors reap rewards? What rewards motivate inventors? Can patents obstruct innovation or liberty? Without patents, how would behavior change? Examples? Ethical issues?

31. The Suit: What is liability? Is it ethical to limit liability? How does behavior change if liability is not limited? What is a public good and who decides? Can "public goods" be bad for the public? Does government substitute free riders? Ethical issues?

32. Doctrinaire: Who owns a life? Does it matter who decides on, or pays for, a physician? What is the difference between licensing and certification? Are open competition and information valuable to good medicine? Examples? Ethical issues?

33. Vice Versa: Are people being harmed? Who and why? Is the law contradictory concerning these activities? Why? What is the difference between disapproving of behavior and outlawing it? Examples? What ethical issues are involved in the use of force?

34. Merryberries: Is it okay to do things that are unhealthy or risky? Should people be required to pay for mistakes of others? When do people learn, or not learn, from mistakes? Are officials wiser than their subjects? Examples? Ethical issues?

35. The Grand Inquirer: What is responsibility? Do people want responsibility? Do people want leaders to make decisions for them? Is choice necessary to have virtue? Is virtue important? Why? Examples? What ethical issues are involved?

36. Loser Law: If innocent people are required to pay for the misfortune of others, how does this affect the behavior of both? Why might people be motivated to feign injury? Does it matter? When is gambling allowed or not allowed? Why? Examples? Ethical issues?

37. The Democracy Gang: Is it okay for one person to take from another by force? Is it okay for majorities to take from minorities by force? What may majorities do that individuals are not allowed to do? How can politics lead to riots? Examples? Ethics?

38. Vultures, Beggars, Con Men, and Kings: What people are symbolized by these: vultures, beggars, con men, or kings? What valuable services do they provide? Should authorities be held to the same rules of behavior as everyone else?

39. Terra Libertas: Is it possible, or desirable, to have a society that is free of force and fraud? Can a vision of utopia be forced upon people? What is the process of discovery in a free society? Can the end justify the means? Examples? Ethical issues?

ACKNOWLEDGEMENTS AND NOTES

I am grateful to many people for their contributions to this project. Sam Slom and Small Business Hawaii are responsible for bringing this publication to life. Flora Ling made fundamental editorial contributions to the writing style and overall presentation of this story. Lucile Schoolland, Nicolai Heering, Fred James, Harry Harrison, Scott Kishimori, and Stuart Hayashi gave meticulous editorial assistance. Randall Lavarias prepared the current illustrations. David Friedman & Tiffany Catalfano drew the lively illustrations in earlier editions. Orlando Valdez provided superb artistic layout and design. Gerhard "Geo" Olsson contributed many philosophical insights and introduced this book to Milton Friedman. Vince Miller and Jim Elwood promoted this book around the world; Louk Jongen, Louis van Gils, Reg Jacklin, Pelle Jensen, Jeff Mallan, and the HPU SIFE team have promoted the book extensively through the Internet.

Hubert & Rita Jongen, Wimmie Albada, and Ton Haggenburg produced the Dutch edition. Dmitrii Costygin and William Milonoff produced the first Russian edition and Kenneth DeGraaf and Elena Mamontova are responsible for the new Russian translation. Linda Tjelta, Jon Henrik Gilhus, and Bent Johan Mosfjell are responsible for the Norwegian editions. Virgis Daukas arranged the Lithuanian edition and uses it regularly in his English language camp along with Monika Lukasiewicz and Stephen Browne. Tomislav Krsmanovic is the great and courageous champion of liberty who has arranged the Serbian, Macedonian, Croatian, Slovenian, Albanian, and Romany editions. Trifun Dimic translated and published the Romany edition. Valentina Buxar translated both Romanian editions and, along with Cris Comanescu, is responsible for the soon-to-be published second Romanian edition. Valdis Bluzma published the Latvian edition. Wilson Ling and Carlos Fernando Souto produced the Portuguese edition. Toshio Murata, Yoko Otsuji, Toyoko Nishimura, Mariko Nakatani, Kayoko Shimpo, and Hiroko Takahashi are responsible for the translation and publication of the Japanese edition by Nippon Hyoron Sha. Alex Heil worked diligently on a translation and Stefan Kopp published the German edition. Jonas Ekebom, Carl Henningsson, Christer Olsson, and Mats Hinze all worked on the Swedish translation and John-Henri Holmberg is preparing it as an e-publication. Jan Jacek Szymona, Jacek Sierpinski, and Andrzej Zwawa produced the Polish editions. Andras Szijjarto is responsible for the Hungarian edition. Judy Nagy translated and published the Spanish edition. Joy-Shan Lam is primarily responsible for the Chinese edition through the *Hong Kong Economic Journal.* Zef Preci, Kozeta Cuadari, and Auron Pasha produced the Albanian edition. Christina Sakaziro Posegate and Winston Posegate produced the Palauan edition. K-mee Jung has been translating the Korean edition. Barun Mitra translated the Bengali edition. Louise Zizka translated the French edition and, with assistance from Patrick Trepanier and Jacques De Guenin, has been energetically seeking a publisher. Aldo Canovari produced the Italian edition. Josef Sima and Radovan Kacin are architects of the Czech edition. Faisal Hassan has translated and arranged for publication of the Somali edition. Andy Nousen has prepared the Esperanto edition. Nellie Manova has prepared the Bulgarian translation. Seig Pedde produced the CD edition.

Many others are currently working on various media editions: Susan Wells, Cindy and Mike Powell, Vanja deJong, and Tracy Ryan. Doug Thorburn, Danute, Venta, & Vytas Barauskas, Lane Yoder, Dick Rowland, and many others have been superb financial supporters of international editions. Additional contributors to this project through ISIL have been: Mark Adamo, Michael Beasley, Glenn Boyer, Charles Branz, Rodger Cosgrove, John Dalhoff, Jean Frissell, Henry Haller III, Thomas Hanlin III, Frank Heemstra, David Hoesly, Douglas Hoiles, Paul Lundberg, Jim McIntosh, Denise & William Murley, Roger Norris, Richard Riemann, Jim Rongstad, David Stiegelmann, Rudy Tietze, Howard Thomson, Susan Wells, and Louise Ziska. Dale Pratt gave encouragement for the original radio broadcasts. Lane Yoder, Nat Mandel, and Bruce Hobbs gave comments and production assistance. Adam Smith, Frederic Bastiat, Milton, Rose, & David Friedman, Ayn Rand, Duncan Scott, Dick Randolph, Henry David Thoreau, Murray Rothbard, Ronald Hamowy, John Goodman, George B. Shaw, Lysander Spooner, Henry Hazlitt, R. W. Grant, Fyodor Dostoyevsky, George Orwell, Jonathan Swift, Lao Tzu, Monty Python, and anonymous office circulars are responsible for inspiring many of the ideas in this fictional text. I owe the deepest gratitude to my parents and grandparents for the development of my personal and philosophical values—especially to my mother for unlimited encouragement. And to my wife Li, I am grateful for her patience, comments, and technical support at difficult times.

RECOMMENDED ORGANIZATIONS

ADVOCATES FOR SELF-GOVERNMENT,
1202 N. Tennessee St. Suite 202, Cartersville, GA 30120, USA
T: 770-386-8372; F: 770-386-8373, www.self-gov.org

CATO INSTITUTE,
1000 Massachusetts Ave. N.W., Washington, D.C., 20001-5403, USA,
T: 202-842-0200, F: 202-842-3490, www.cato.org

FOUNDATION FOR ECONOMIC EDUCATION,
30 South Broadway, Irvington, NY 10533, USA.
T: 914-591-7230; F: 914-591-8910; www.fee@fee.org

FREEDOMS FOUNDATION AT VALLEY FORGE,
1601 Valley Forge, Valley Forge, PA 19482, USA,
Tel. 610-933-8825, Fax 610-935-0522, www.ffvf.org

FUTURE OF FREEDOM FOUNDATION,
11350 Random Hills Road, Suite 800, Fairfax VA, 22030, USA,
Tel. 703-934-6101, Fax 703-352-8678, www.fff.org

INSTITUTE FOR HUMANE STUDIES,
George Mason University, 3401 N. Fairfax Drive, Arlington, VA 22201-4432, USA
T: 703-993-4880 or 800-697-8799, F: 703-993-4890, www.TheIHS.org

INTERNATIONAL SOCIETY FOR INDIVIDUAL LIBERTY,
836-B Southampton Rd. Suite 299, Benicia, CA, 94510, USA,
T: 415-864-0952, F: 415-864-7506, www.isil.org

LAISSEZ FAIRE BOOKS,
942 Howard St., San Francisco, CA 94103, USA,
T: 415-541-9780, Toll-free: 800-326-0996, F: 415-541-0597, www.laissezfaire.org

LIBERTY MAGAZINE & FOUNDATION
1018 Water St., Suite 201, Port Townsend, WA 98368,
E-mail: rwbradford@bigfoot.com

LUDWIG VON MISES INSTITUTE
518 W. Magnolia Avenue, Auburn, Alabama 36832-4528
T: 334-321-2100, F: 334-321-2119, www.mises.org

THE OBJECTIVIST CENTER
11 Raymond Ave., Suite 31, Poughkeepsie, NY 12603
T: 914-471-6100, F: 914-471-6195, toc@objectivistcenter.org

REASON MAGAZINE & FOUNDATION
3445 S. Sepulveda Blvd., Suite 400, Los Angeles, CA, 90034, USA,
T:310-391-2245, F: 310-391-4395, www.reason.org

STOSSEL IN THE CLASSROOM
THE PALMER R. CHITESTER FUND,
9008 Main Place, Suite #3, McKean , PA, 16426
T: 888-242-0563; F: 814-476-1283, www.prcfund.org/stossel/

RECOMMENDED READING

Bastiat, Frederic, *The Law*
Burris, Alan, *A Liberty Primer*
Friedman, David, *The Machinery of Freedom*
Friedman, Milton & Rose, *Free to Choose*
Grant, R.W., *The Incredible Bread Machine*
Hazlitt, Henry, *Economics in One Lesson*
Rand, Ayn, *Atlas Shrugged*
Rothbard, Murray, *For a New Liberty*
Ruwart, Mary, *Healing Our World*
Tannehill, Linda & Morris, *The Market for Liberty*
Thoreau, Henry David, *On the Duty of Civil Disobedience*

For additional copies of this book, contact:
Small Business Hawaii,
Hawaii Kai Corporate Plaza, 6600 Kalanianaole Hwy., Suite 212,
Honolulu, Hawaii, 96825,

T: 808-396-1724, F: 808-396-1726, sbh@lava.net

www.smallbusinesshawaii.org

INTERNATIONAL EDITIONS

Russian, Dutch, Norwegian, Lithuanian, Romanian, Serbian, Croatian, Macedonian, Slovenian, German, Spanish, Palauan, Chinese, Albanian, Latvian, Portuguese, Hungarian, Italian, Romany, Czech, Polish, and Japanese

"It certainly presents basic economic principles in a very simple and intelligible form. It is an imaginative and very useful piece of work."
—Milton Friedman, *Nobel laureate in economics*

"My notions of education previously consisted of threadbare textbooks, stern and cold teachers, of sweating...I have realized that this book is the best textbook I have ever come across...I have learnt more about free markets, private property, free flow of ideas, people and goods, than during the whole of my studies, both at high school and now at the university."
—Valerija Dasic, *Belgrade, Serbia*

"...[A] fine book for promoting free market ideas for young people..."
—Karl Hess, *author of Capitalism for Kids*

"Your book is utterly fabulous! It is a Johnny Appleseed of liberty."
—Vince Miller, *President, International Society for Individual Liberty*

"It's great!...I could see the influence of Bastiat, von Mises, and Pat Paulsen."
—Gene Berkman, *owner Renaissance Books*

"The free market principles discussed are valuable for everyone who is interested in creating a free society."
—Virginijus Daukas, *President, Free Market Foundation, Lithuania*

"...[I]t is, perhaps, the most clearly written and thus readily understandable presentation of the all too neglected philosophical legacy of Liberty and Free Market Economics that I have ever read."
—Nicolai Heering, *member of Libertas Society, Denmark*

"...[A] very impressive book. When more and more of the younger generation are attracted to comic books, animation, and illustrated books, your approach is one of the best means to promote our philosophy."

—Prof. Toshio Murata, *President, Yokohama College of Commerce, translator of Human Action, by Ludwig von Mises, Japan*

"It is a great inspiration...!"

—Mats Hinze, *co-founder of Tritnaha, Sweden*

"[The book] makes you laugh, but it leaves you meditating, which is one of the most effective ways ever invented...in making them understand the principles of a free market economy and a free society."

—Valentina Buxar, *Fundatia Liberala, Romania*

" Ideological topics that otherwise would require books to read and years to debate are made clear in five minutes. I plan to send copies to all branches of the Free Democrats...."

—Jon Henrik Gilhus, *International Secretary, Free Democrats, Norway*

"...[W]e used [it] to teach the principles of freedom."

—Hubert Jongen, *Chairman, Dutch Libertarian Centre, Holland*

"Thank you, thank you, thank you for that wonderful book! It was very refreshing to read a book so logical, entertaining, and enlightening. ...The story may be set in a fantasy world, but the situations involved come way too close to reality. Again, thank you for the wonderful book!"

—Stuart Hayashi, *1999 Valedictorian, Mililani High School, Hawaii*

"I'm simply amazed by your book: The Adventures of Jonathan Gullible. To tell you the truth I'm also a bit scared of your accuracy and sharpness...I couldn't help but thinking how long you'd been in Poland! It's just unbelievable—when I was reading the book I thought—this is just like going back in time, before 1989."

—Monika Lukasiewicz, *Drama Director, Liberty English Camp, Warszawa, Poland*

THE AUTHOR: Ken Schoolland is presently an associate professor of economics and political science at Hawaii Pacific University. Prior to that, he was the Director of the Master of Science in Japanese Business Studies program at Chaminade University of Honolulu and head of the Business and Economics Program at Hawaii Loa College.

Following his graduate studies at Georgetown University, he served as an international economist in the U.S. International Trade Commission, the U.S. Department of Commerce, and on assignment to the White House, Office of the Special Representative for Trade Negotiations.

Schoolland left government for the field of education, teaching business and economics at Sheldon Jackson College in Alaska. He also taught at Hakodate University in Japan and wrote, *Shogun's Ghost: The Dark Side of Japanese Education*, which has been published in English and in Japanese.

Schoolland is a member of the Board of Directors for the International Society for Individual Liberty and is a Sam Walton Fellow for Students in Free Enterprise.

THE ILLUSTRATOR: Randall Lavarias was born and raised in Waialua, Oahu and is the second youngest of seven children. His parents are second generation Filipino Americans. His father was a cane haul driver for Waialua Sugar Company and his mother worked at the Del Monte Cannery. At the age of 4, Randall began drawing and his dad, also an artist, inspired him to become an illustrator.

Lavarias took art classes from the University of Hawaii and Kapiolani Community College and he earned an AS degree in Commercial Art from Honolulu Community College. Later he worked for a variety of graphic agencies including Commercial Graphics, Polynesian Prints, and Crazy Shirts. As a free lance artist, he has done most of his work for companies making T-shirts, brochures, and magazines. As an illustrator, his main interest is in creating drawings that are realistic and expressive.

THE PUBLISHER: Sam Slom, President of Small Business Hawaii (SBH), a 501(c)(6) non-profit corporation, dedicated to improving Hawaii's business climate while promoting, educating, and effectively representing more than 2,500 independent small businesses statewide since 1976, is a private consulting economist in Honolulu, economic educator, and president/owner of SMS Consultants. He has been quoted in national publications including, *Forbes, The Economist, Money, USA Today, The Washington Post, The Wall Street Journal,* and *Investor's Business Daily.*

In 1996 he was elected as a Republican to the State Senate (8th–Waialae Iki, Aina Haina, Niu, Hawaii Kai), serving as Minority Floor Leader and member of the Commerce & Consumer Protection, Economic Development, Education & Technology, Labor & Environment, Transportation & Intergovernmental Affairs Committees; Joint Long Term Care Financing and Joint Legislative Committee on Early Childhood Education and co-chair of the Legislative Small Business Caucus. Re-elected in 2000 and chosen Senate Minority Leader, he is a member of the Ways & Means, Judiciary, Economic Development, Tourism, and Labor Committees.